Violets Are Blue

By Elizabeth Rose

NASHVILLE

© 2012 by Elizabeth Rose

Published by THE KOOKOGEY GROUP,

9050 Carothers Pkwy, Suite 104, #25, Franklin, TN 37067

www.kookogey.com

The KOOKOGEY name and logo are trademarks of THE KOOKOGEY GROUP, registration pending in the United States Patent & Trademark Office.

Elizabeth Rose is a 14-year-old author from Franklin, Tennessee. The oldest of six home-schooled children, she launched her first blog (www.lizzyslovelylibrary.blogspot.com) at age 12. *Violets are Blue* is her first book. To learn more, please visit 365daysoftitanic.blogspot.com.

Cover Design:
Elizabeth Rose

Special thanks to Jordan Mattison and Marc Theodosiou

Manufactured in the United States of America

ISBN: 978-1475090055

This book is dedicated to my family. Thank you for supporting my writing ambitions ever since I was a little girl. Thank you for always being my source of strength throughout the entirety of this process. And most of all, thank you for not being afraid to tell me when something needed to be changed or fixed. This book is the result of your constant dedication and love.

CHAPTER 1

I never liked the water very much, at least not the water I knew. It was dark, dense, and deep. I much preferred dry land. There was something firm about dry land—I could trust it. Water changed all the time, lapping against the shore, pulling back again, rising and falling with the tide. Water was fickle and uncertain.

My best friend, Lillian, did not agree with me. She loved the water, and when we were very young, she could nearly always be found dripping wet. I couldn't understand her joy at diving into the freezing cold ocean every chance she got; what could she possibly see in it?

"Come, Vi," she would beg, splashing into the water. "It's wonderful—you don't know what you're missing!"

"Oh, yes I do," I insisted from my comfortable spot on an old quilt laid out on the sand. "You go. I'm quite content to sit here and read." And I would turn back to my book while she frolicked in the ocean waves.

Perhaps if we'd lived in a warmer place, I would have liked the ocean better. But that wasn't the case. We lived in Eastbourne, a small resort town located in East Sussex, Great Britain. And although it was known as one of the sunniest places in England, the warmest it ever got was seventy degrees. Gorgeous, perfect weather for wandering along the sandy shores. But swimming? Absurd.

Lillian knew each time she begged that I swim with her that I would refuse, but she still asked. I think she held a small, secret hope that one day I would join her. And even if I didn't go, I could never return home without getting at least a little wet. My friend seemed to have some idea that if I wouldn't come to the ocean, she would bring the ocean to me. Whether it was by dumping a pail of water on me or hugging me when she was drenched, she somehow managed to get me wet every time. I would pretend to be cross, but it never came as much of a surprise when Lilli poured seawater over my head. It was just her way of teasing me.

One time, she was creeping up behind me with a full pail of water as I lay on my quilt on the beach. I could hear her footsteps in the soft sand, but she didn't know it. Right before she lifted the pail to soak me (and my book), I turned around and said calmly, "Oh, hello."

I will never forget Lilli's face at that moment. Her green eyes were like huge, round discs, and she nearly jumped a foot. Of course, in doing so, she lost most of the water in her pail as it flew onto her, dousing her hair and face and dress thoroughly. I watched her standing there, shivering and dripping in the water that was meant for me, and couldn't resist a giggle. Always good-natured, Lillian smiled as well.

"I'm sure I must look like a silly goose now," she said ruefully.

"Oh no," I said assuredly. "You look *much* better."

It was June, 1911. I was fourteen years old—nearly a young lady. I was just coming to the age where I would be expected to act like a woman, wearing long skirts. In less than a year, when I turned fifteen, I would have to start wearing a corset. My older sister, Emma, had been wearing a corset for a year now, and it did not look pleasant. I was dreading the time when I would be chained to such horrid garments.

Sitting on the doorstep of my family's boarding house, I watched people stroll down the walk. A woman was walking with her child, and the little boy was grinning as he stumbled along, assisted by his mother. She was pointing to the ships in the harbor, and his smile grew wider with each vessel they passed. Tourists were always enamored with the beauty of Eastbourne, and I couldn't blame them. I loved my home dearly.

The one I fondly thought of as "my beach" stretched between the Pier and the Wish Tower. This was where our boarding house was located. Another one of the beaches, Falling Sands, was a tranquil spot located at the foot of the infamous Beachy Head, near the South Downs. Many a person was known to commit suicide by leaping from the chalky cliff one hundred and sixty-two meters to the sea below. Guards patrolled the Head

4

night and day in an attempt to stop these desperate souls, but the death rates did not seem to change. A very small part of me wanted to catch a glimpse up close of the notorious cliff, but the nearest Mum allowed me to it were pictures in the newspaper.

Among all the attractions of my hometown, the most popular spot was the Eastbourne pier, visible from Beachy Head and walking distance from our boarding house. Jutting a full three hundred meters into the ocean, the seaside pleasure pier boasted a movie cinema, camera obscura, and office suite, among others. It was a rich and luxurious place, quite the opposite of our humble home. On my birthday every year, Mum and Father would take me to the Pier, and we would share a treat together. Last year, when I turned fourteen, Father had treated us to a moving picture in the cinema. This special experience would remain with me for the rest of my life.

Next to the Pier were the Carpet Gardens. These world famous gardens were truly a site to behold. Gorgeous flowers, rocks, and rare tropical blossoms filled the air with a heavenly perfume. I had begged

Mum to take me there every chance I could when I was young, but I was not allowed to go nearly as often as I would have liked. Mum's answer to my pleading was either "No, dear, I must hang out the laundry," or "Vi, I must feed your sister, I can't take you now." Sometimes Mum would send Emma with me, and my older sister would sit on one of the benches while I walked up and down the beds in a silent rapture. Flowers would always be close to my heart.

I paused in my daydreaming for a moment, pulled back to reality by the sighting of two strange men amidst all the beauty and pleasure. Staggering down the road, they laughed and joked, seeming not to notice anyone around them.

They must be drunk, I though disgustedly.

To my dismay, the intoxicated men began to make their way toward our boarding house. One of the men, a tall lean one with blonde hair, pointed at me and whispered something to his companion, who guffawed loudly. I stood immediately with my hands on my hips, attempting to block the doorway, but they just pushed right past me.

6

"Out of our way, girl," the tall man said with slurred speech. "We need to get through."

"My mother does not accept boarders such as yourself," I said sternly, surprised at my own bravery.

"Does she not, eh?" the second man said. He was short and stout, with oily black hair.

"No." I glared at them, hoping that if I was forceful enough, they would leave. But the men just laughed rudely again and pushed past me, entering the boarding house.

"Where's yer mum?" they insisted.

I attempted to buy time. "Not here."

The tall man laughed brashly. "We can see that! That's why we're asking where she *is*."

"I don't know," I muttered.

"Insolent girl," the stout man almost shouted. "Can't even tell us where her own mum is! I'd better go and find the lady myself."

"No!" I said instantly. "I mean... I just remembered where she is. I'll go and get her." I was about to leave the sitting room, but turned once more to face the two men. "Wait here," I insisted. The blonde

7

man just smirked and leaned against the fireplace. The stout man was sprawled across the sofa, inspecting his boots.

Mum was out back behind the boarding house, washing laundry in buckets of hot soapy water. Her slight form was bent with weariness, and I watched her brush a few strands of damp hair out of her eyes.

"What is it, Vi?" she asked me, without looking up from her work. "Are you finished with the dusting?"

It took me all of two seconds to recall that she had asked me to do the dusting nearly twenty minutes ago.

I must've forgotten, I though with chagrin.

"Mum, there are two men in the parlor. They want rooms."

"Tell them I'll be there in a moment," she replied, her back still turned to me. "I need to hang this last sheet on the line."

"Mum, they're not the most... *clean* characters," I said, struggling for the proper words.

"Don't worry about footprints," she said to me calmly. "Soap and water can work miracles, Vi, especially after they leave. We need the money."

By now she had finished wringing the water out of the bed sheet. Several large puddles of water had pooled next to the tub, and they were swiftly becoming mud in the soft dirt. I observed my mother as she struggled to get the sheet over the line without dirtying it once more. She held a clothespin in her mouth as she lifted the heavy sheet with both hands and draped it over the line that was strung between the house and a large tree. Holding it steady with one hand, Mum removed the clothespin from her mouth and secured the sheet. It billowed in the warm summer breeze, blowing droplets in my direction. I jumped out of the way so as not to get wet.

"Now then, Violet," Mum said, her hands on her hips. "Let's see about those boarders."

I followed her into the house, picking my way carefully around the mud puddles.

Emma met us at the back door, wiping her hands on a damp dishtowel.

"Mum, there are some men in the parlor—"

"Violet told me," Mum said calmly. "Don't worry yourself over a little dirt. It's the price we pay for running a boarding house."

"Mum, they're *drunk!*" Emma blurted out.

"*Drunk?!*" Mum gasped. Her face was shocked. "Violet, why didn't you tell me? Drunk men—in my home!"

"Mum, I tried to tell you, but—"

"Oh, never mind!" Emma interrupted impatiently. "Mum, they're touching the china teacups in the cupboard!"

Mum pushed past Emma and me quickly, and we followed her to the sitting room. The stout man was passed out on the couch, and the blonde man was pulling our nice teacups out of the cupboard. He held one carelessly; I realized in distress that it was one that had belonged to my great grandmother.

"Sir, please put that down," Mum said firmly, her voice only wavering a bit. "It is of great value."

The man placed the teacup on the edge of the table quickly, and we all let out our breath audibly in a

10

chorus of sighs. But, as he turned quickly toward the rest of the china in the cupboard, he bumped the cup. I watched in suppressed horror as it was knocked swiftly from the precarious position on the edge of the table. Mum leaped to catch it, but her fingers missed the shattering china. In a matter of seconds, a well of memories was dashed to the ground. Tears came to my eyes swiftly, but I fought to hold them back. I wasn't going to let these awful men see me cry.

In his drunken stupor, the man did not seem to realize that he had bumped the cup. Mum took the other teacup from his hand swiftly and closed the cupboard door firmly. Opening the front door, she motioned for the men to leave. The dark-haired man stood now, awakened from his sleep by the crash of china against the wood floor.

"Whas goin' on?" he asked sleepily.

"You and your friend are leaving. *Now.*" Mum's voice was as stern as it had been less than a week ago when she had caught my six year old brother, Henry, sticking his finger in the jam jar.

"C'mon, Joe," the lean man said, pulling his friend along.

The two men stumbled out the door and down the street. Only after Mum had closed the door and locked it tightly did we all breathe freely once more.

"That's it," Mum said firmly. "I won't cater to such characters, and I won't have them around my children either! The idea!"

"But, Mum," I objected. "We need the money—you said so yourself. We can't help who stays here."

"Oh yes we can," she replied. "Because no stranger will be staying under my roof ever again."

CHAPTER 2

I couldn't fall asleep that night. Mum and Father were up late talking, and I tossed and turned, hearing the murmur of their voices in the background. My covers felt heavy, and I pushed them away; moments later, I was yanking the sheets back up to my chin, shivering. Was I sick? Placing a hand to my sweaty forehead, I tried to determine whether I had a fever. I didn't feel any warmer than normal. My stomach churned with nervousness. What were Mum and Father talking about? And what on earth did Mum mean by "no stranger will be staying under my roof ever again"?

Finally, I gave up on trying to sleep. Slipping out of bed quietly so as to not awaken Emma, I tiptoed down the hall to my parents' bedroom. I couldn't hear voices anymore, only the sound of deep, even breathing that came through the door. They were asleep.

I raised my hand to knock on the bedroom door, but paused. I hated to awaken them. Instead, I made myway further down the hall to the staircase, and then down to the kitchen. Filling the tea kettle with water, I set it on the stove to boil. I felt like a cup of tea.

"Violet," someone murmured from behind me. The voice was sleepy.

I turned to see Mum standing in the doorway.

"Why are you up, dear?" she asked.

"I couldn't sleep."

Mum was silent for a while. The only sound in the still room was the quiet bubbling of the boiling water. The pot began to steam. I took it off the stove and prepared the tea quietly.

"Violet..." Mum said softly. She stroked my cheek.

"What is it, Mum?" I asked curiously.

"Vi, we're going to America."

"To-to America?" I gasped, not believing. "You mean—to visit?"

"No, dear," she answered sadly. "To live."

All the air in my body seemed to go out.

14

I could barely remember a time when I had not known Lilli: we had been friends nearly our whole lives. Mum and Mrs. Prescott were like sisters to each other, and Mr. Prescott could often be found discussing news and politics with Father. The Prescotts only had three children; besides Lilli, they had a son and another daughter. The latter was just seven years old; a very pretty and shy little girl with the same straight blonde hair and green eyes as her elder sister. Their son, Will, who was three years my senior, was a good friend of Emma's. A *very* good friend.

Mrs. Prescott had dark hair that she often pulled back neatly in a bun. I loved being around her, for she reminded me so much of my own mum. Lilli's mother was small and slight of figure, barely taller than her oldest daughter. I couldn't recall her ever speaking a harsh word to anyone. Mr. Prescott, however, was tall and strong, with a great booming laugh that could be heard from all the way down the street. Like his wife, he also had dark hair, with a beard and moustache that he kept neatly trimmed. He often spent evenings by the fire with his newspaper and his smoking pipe.

Will was tall and lean, with dark curly hair. He often joked and teased us girls, and as a young child, I found his blunt manner aggravating. When a small lad, he was forever placing spiders in the cream pitchers or slipping chunks of ice down our dresses. The only girl who was safe from his tricks was my sister, Emma. For some reason, he never teased her nearly as much as he did the rest of us. Now that he was nearly grown—he would be seventeen in October—Will refrained from most of these childish tricks, but he still teased occasionally. Still, Emma was his good friend, and they spent much time together, taking walks and keeping up lively conversations. I often wondered what it was that they were saying to each other, but Emma would never tell me and only told me to mind my own business.

But Lillian was my special friend. We were kindred spirits, and would be, I assumed, for the rest of our lives. To the outside world, we didn't seem very alike. Lillian had medium-length, straight blonde hair

16

that was always falling out of braids. Her eyes were a mix between grey and green, and nearly always happy. She was a joyful and carefree girl. Virtually nothing bothered her, and the little that did was soon resolved. I, on the other hand, had curly blonde hair that I kept in a bun most of the time. My eyes were a dark, deep blue with hints of grey—the color of the ocean before a storm. My personality was a strange mix—quiet and thoughtful, but with quick temper. I didn't like to show my emotions, and was extremely private.

Because of our differences, we fit each other perfectly. Lilli's docile nature balanced out my fiery temper, and my thoughtful mind was the perfect match to her flighty spirit. We both enjoyed reading and devoured books rapidly. We shared a love for babies and little children—Lillian especially. She hoped to have many children when she was grown and married. We told each other everything; we could even finish each other's sentences. We were so close—it didn't even seem probable that something would happen to pull us apart.

Father informed all of us of the pending move at the breakfast table a few days later. The rest of the children seemed to take the news remarkably well. Robert, my nine year old brother, was especially excited because we would be crossing the ocean on a ship. He was eagerly questioning Father about the fine details of our voyage, as if completely ignorant of the fact that we were leaving the only home we'd ever known.

Emma was the only one to show some sort of emotion that was not excited when Father made his announcement. Her eyes grew wide with shock and sorrow, and a hand flew to her throat.

"*Leaving?*" she asked, her voice cracking. "We're leaving *Eastbourne?*"

"Yes, dear," Mum said, stroking her eldest daughter's hand. "Your father and I don't feel comfortable raising you children in such unreliable circumstances. We have never had disreputable characters come to the boarding house before, but after the incident on Tuesday..." Her voice trailed off.

Emma seemed to be holding back tears. Her voice was unsteady as she asked to be excused. Mum nodded her head, and I watched my sister leave the room.

At least she understands, I thought bitterly. No one else seemed to care. The rest of my siblings were actually *excited* about this move. *Aren't they sad to leave their friends at school? What about our church?* I gulped. *What about Lilli?*

I didn't want to think about her at this moment, so I tried to speak cheerfully as I asked Mum, "When will we depart?"

"As soon as your father can arrange tickets for us on a ship that is leaving soon," Mum said. "Two weeks, at most."

Two weeks. The words were like chains. Just two more weeks of happiness.

How would I tell Lilli?

CHAPTER 3

"I... I don't understand." For once, Lilli didn't have a huge smile on her face. Two little tears trickled down her cheek. "How can you be leaving?"

"Mum and Father don't want us to be keeping close quarters with any unwholesome people."

"Then close the boarding house!"

"We *can't,* Lilli. How else would we live?" I felt like I was explaining something to a small child.

"Well, how do you plan to live in—where is it you're going?"

"New York. And Father says he'll try to find carpentry work. I guess there's more need for carpenters in America than here."

"Can't they go and leave you here? You could live with us." Lilli's voice was desperate.

"I don't think Mum would allow that. Besides, I would miss them dreadfully. How would *you* like to live here while your family moved to America?"

"I don't think I'd like that," Lillian admitted. "But it'll be nearly as bad if you're leaving. How will I live?"

"As long as your heart is still beating, you'll be able to live just fine," I commented dryly.

"You know what I mean." She leaned her head on my shoulder. "I'll be physically living, but I won't be able to enjoy anything with you gone."

"That's not true," I tried to protest. "You have lots of friends."

"Yes..." she said slowly. "But I don't have any other friends like you."

A few tears fell from my eyes without my consent, dampening my apron. We were quiet for a while.

"Are you girls all right?" I heard Mrs. Prescott ask from behind the door.

Lilli sniffed and wiped her nose. "Yes, we're fine, Mum," she replied quickly.

21

"Lillian, dear, I want you to take the sheets off your bed so I can wash them," Lilli's mother reminded.

"Yes, ma'am," Lilli said dutifully. "Will you help me, Vi?"

We rose from our seats on the edge of the bed and began to remove the quilts and sheets.

"How much longer?" Lilli asked quietly. She didn't have to say anything more—I knew what she meant.

"Mum said no more than two weeks. She wants us to leave as soon as possible."

"And your father?"

"He agrees with Mum."

Lilli sighed. "That means we have only two more weeks together. Do you think you'll ever come back to visit?"

"I don't know... It's an expensive journey, and not one that can be made often. I may never—"

"—see you again," she interrupted, finishing my sentence sadly.

"Will you write me?" I asked.

"Every day!" she replied eagerly.

"Really?" I asked skeptically, taking the pillowcase off of her pillow. "*Every* day?"

"Well, I'll try, anyway. Will you write me?"

"Of course I will." I threw the pillow at Lilli. "You know that."

"You mustn't leave out anything," she insisted, catching the pillow. "I want to hear just what life is like in New York."

"And I want to hear about everything that is going on here in Eastbourne," I replied, "even if you say the same thing a dozen times."

It is surprising how quickly time flies when you're busy. Mum had us all on out toes, packing necessary things and selling what we would not need to take with us. Before I knew it, two weeks had flown by, and we would be leaving early the next morning.

It was about two o' clock in the afternoon. Grace, my youngest sister, was taking her afternoon nap, but the rest of us were packing up the house with Mum. A slow drizzle of rain fell outside, making the house seem cozy and warm. I had just finished emptying the cupboards in the kitchen, and was cautiously dragging the heavy trunk into Mum and Father's bedroom, where the rest of the filled trunks were being temporarily kept.

"You did remember to pack newspaper around our dishes, didn't you?" Mum asked me. "I don't want them breaking."

"Yes, Mum, I remembered the newspaper," I sighed. "The dishes will be fine."

"Good," Mum said. "Is there anything else that needs to be packed in the kitchen?"

"Yes, the table and chairs."

"Father said he will make new ones when we get to New York. It's too much of a hassle to take them on the ship."

"Speaking of ships, on what ship will we be sailing, Mum?" Robert asked curiously, looking up from the pile of folded shirts he was packing in an open trunk.

"I don't know her name," Mum answered slowly. "But she's not very big. Your father couldn't afford for us to sail on a fine ocean liner.

24

"Aww..." Robert and Henry groaned in unison. "I was hoping we could go on the *Olympic*," Robert added, mentioning a new ocean liner that was just being launched.

"Robert, that's one of the finest ships in the world!" my ten-year-old sister Helen said incredulously.

"How could we afford even a third class ticket?" Helen's twin, Anna, added.

"Girls, don't mock him," Mum reprimanded gently. "I won't have my children teasing each other for honest mistakes. Now Robert," she said, turning to her son. "It is true that we wouldn't be able to afford a ticket—even a third class one—on such a ship. We simply don't have the funds right now."

Robert hung his head in disappointment. "Will we *ever* have the funds?"

"Perhaps one day," Mum said lightly. "And even if we as a family don't, you may be able to cross the ocean on a fine ship like the *Olympic* when you are grown. There is a time for everything and a season for every activity under heaven.'"

"Is that from the Bible?" Anna asked curiously.

"Yes," Mum replied. "It's from Ecclesiastes, chapter three, verse one. Now children, we've spent enough time chattering away about ships. Let us get back to our work. Vi, I believe Emma may need your help. She's in your bedroom packing clothes."

"Yes, Mum," I said obediently, leaving the room.

I found Emma in our bedroom, just as Mum had said, but she was not packing clothes. Instead, she was sitting on the window seat, watching the rain drizzle down the pane, her back to me.

"Emma?" I said quietly.

"Yes?" she answered without turning around. She continued to stare out the window, her shoulders slumped.

"Are—are you all right?" I asked, concerned. She did not seem her usual self.

"I'm fine, Violet," Emma replied quickly, turning around this time. But her tear-stained cheeks and red eyes spoke volumes.

"Mum said you were packing our clothes," I said.

Emma looked at the open trunk on our bed, less than half-filled with the skirts, gowns, and undergarments that lay in neat stacks next to it.

"I guess I got distracted," she answered dully, rising from her seat. "I should finish my task. Why did Mum send you in here?"

I joined my sister by the bed, helping her pile the clothes into the trunk, packing them tightly so that they wouldn't jolt about when we were on the ship. "She wanted me to help you with the packing. I finished emptying the kitchen shelves."

"Oh." Emma's voice was uninterested.

"Emma, do you have a fever?"

"Of course not," my sister replied automatically. "Why ever would you think such a thing?"

"You don't seem well."

"I am perfectly healthy," she tried to assure me.

"No, you're not!" I contradicted. "You may be well in body, but you are certainly not well in spirit. Emma, when I came in here, you were not packing and you looked as though you had been crying. Now you are despondent, and not at all like your usual cheery self. What is *wrong?*"

She sighed, then sat down on the bed. I waited anxiously for her to speak.

"It's... it's this whole moving nonsense. We're going to Southampton tomorrow; the day after that we set sail! America, Violet. New York! It's so far away from everything... every*one*..." Her voice trailed off for a moment, and a few more tears fell from her eyes.

"And by "everyone," you mean a certain lad by the name of Will Prescott?"

Emma blushed and tossed her head. "Of course not. Don't speak such utter nonsense, Vi. Naturally, I will miss all of the Prescotts, and every other family we are acquainted with here in Eastbourne." She wiped her cheeks once more and smoothed her hair. "Now then, shall we get on with our work?" she said briskly. "Mum must be wondering what could be taking us so long."

I merely nodded and continued to pack the garments into the trunk. But I hadn't forgotten that slight color that rose to her cheeks upon the mentioning of Will Prescott's name.

28

"Violet, Emma, wake up."

Mum's voice roused me from my sleep. Opening my eyes sleepily, I yawned and looked around. Our room was still dark. *It must be very early in the morning,* I thought. Mum shook Emma one last time to wake her, then left to awaken the other children.

"Come, Vi," Emma said sleepily, sitting up and stretching. "We mustn't be late for the train." She nudged me gently, then slipped out of bed to get dressed.

I yawned once more, savoring my last moments in my own bed. Mum had lit a single candle in our room, and I watched it flicker and dance. Our curtains had been drawn for the night, and remained drawn now, since we would not be returning to our home. Still, I knew behind the folds of cloth the sky was as dark as night. I had never been up this early before. There was a quiet stillness to the house—and, I sensed, to all of Eastbourne—that only occurred in the very early hours of the morning. I wanted to snuggle back down under my covers and sleep for several more hours, until I would be awoken naturally by the golden sunlight streaming through the curtains Mum always opened right before we woke. I wanted to wake to Emma singing as she dressed. I wanted to smell the delicious scent of pancakes frying as Mum made breakfast. I wanted everything to be normal, as it had always been every day of my life. But it wasn't. I was waking to a dark morning—the morning I would leave my home for good—and I needed to get up quickly and get dressed, lest we miss the train that was to take all of us to Southampton.

Finally, with a resigned sigh, I got out of bed. We had each laid out our clothes on the ends of our beds the night before, and now I reached for my plain grey skirt and white blouse. Already dressed, Emma was twisting her long dark hair into a simple bun.

When I had finished dressing and braiding my hair, we slowly took the sheets off of our bed. I tried to make the task last as long as it could, for the longer it took, the longer until I had to leave. Emma took extra care folding the sheets, and I smoothed the quilt until nary a wrinkle could be found, but we could delay no longer. Already, Father was calling that it was time to leave. I glanced mournfully around the small room I had shared with my sister for as long as I could remember, Emma blew out the candle, and we left the room, closing the door behind us.

The rest of the family was gathered in the sitting room, waiting for us. Helen opened her mouth to complain about how long Emma and I had been, but Father shushed her quickly. I handed the folded bedclothes to Mum without a word, and she quietly placed them in the last trunk, closing the lid over our belongings.

A soft drizzle was falling outside as we all stepped into the waiting automobile that would take us to the train station. I paused before climbing in to look one last time at my dearly beloved home.

"Come, Violet," Father said gently.

Reluctantly, I climbed into the automobile. Father was the last to get in, and he closed the door behind himself. Slowly, the car made its way down the streets, and our house disappeared from view in the rain.

A few tears fell from my eyes and streamed down my cheeks. Mum saw my damp face and squeezed my hand.

"It's all right, Vi," she said soothingly. "You'll like New York. You'll see."

I wasn't convinced that I would like New York, but my mother's gentle voice calmed me a little.

Lillian and all the rest of the Prescotts were waiting for us at the train station. They were waiting to say goodbye.

"Oh Lilli," I said through my tears. "How will I manage without you?"

"As long as your heart is beating, you'll manage just fine," she answered with a small smile, but her eyes were sad.

"You will write me, won't you?" I said urgently.

"Of course," Lilli assured me. "And you must remember to write me as well."

"I will, I will," I promised.

Next to us, Mum and Mrs. Prescott were exchanging goodbyes as well.

"You must send us word as soon as you are settled in New York," Mrs. Prescott insisted.

"Of course, Amelia." Mum seemed to be struggling to keep the tears from falling.

"Father, the train's here!" Henry said. We all turned to see the train pull into the station, screeching as it came to a stop.

"I guess... you need to leave," Lillian said reluctantly.

"I guess I do."

"Don't forget me, Violet."

"How could I forget you? You're my best friend in the whole world."

"Surely not," she said quietly, looking down.

"Yes," I said, looking at her closely. "You are. Don't you ever forget that."

"We need to go—the train is waiting," Father said solemnly. He shook hands with Mr. Prescott, and then the children and he began to board the train. Mum hugged Mrs. Prescott, then she went with Father, carrying Grace. I squeezed Lilli's hand one last time, then followed the rest of my family. Emma was the last

33

to board the train, looking back at the Prescotts reluctantly. As soon as she was on board, the train began to pick up speed. The people in the station backed away from the tracks, so as not to be in any danger from the heavy locomotive. Slowly and steadily, we began to move out of the station. I watched Lilli's face as we moved further and further down the track, her eyes full of unshed tears.

Then I looked back at the rest of my family, all seated cozily together on the train. Anna was leaning her head on Mum's shoulder, and Mum was stroking her hair. Father was telling the boys about the mechanisms and inner workings of a train, and Robert especially was listening eagerly, eyes alight. Emma was holding little Grace on her lap, singing a lullaby in hushed tones.

Despite my sadness at all I had just left behind me in Eastbourne, I managed a small smile. Emma noticed it, and she smiled back.

CHAPTER 4

In some ways, life was very different in America, and in other ways, it was no different than in had been at home in Eastbourne. Our normal schedules were the same, but our surroundings never failed to change things just enough so that I always felt out of place, as if I was teetering on the edge of a tightrope between England and America, belonging to neither and an outsider to both.

In New York, I awoke in the mornings to carts rattling down the busy streets; to peddlers calling to other peddlers and to possible customers. The noises were something that tended to annoy me. *Why,* I thought, *do I have to awaken to such noises and sounds? Is it not enough that I have to live here? Am I to have the worst experience possible?* My questions always went unanswered.

As usual, Emma was already out of bed when I woke up. My neat and orderly sister had packed away any emotion that had revealed itself on that train ride from Eastbourne to Southampton, and she was now as she had always been before: perfectly sensible and reliable, without getting carried away by her fears or uncertainties. We could not have been more different.

Rising from my bed at last, I straightened the sheets quickly and fluffed my one pillow. Traveling to New York had taken all of our means. We were, in a sense, poor as church mice. Father worked to earn all the income he could to support us, but seven children took a lot of supporting. Mum spoke every now and then, in a wistful tone, of a time when she could replace her worn-out apron with a new one. My sisters and I had secretly planned to pool our money in order to get her that apron, but our money was scarce, and we were not going to near our goal for quite some time.

I leaned out of my bedroom window, my golden curls blowing free in the breeze. I noticed a small red rose growing from a forgotten window box. *It must be left over from when this building was new,* I thought, plucking it. The deep red of the rose was my favorite color; the depth of its brilliant hue seemed to satisfy some craving in my heart in a way other colors couldn't. My eldest sister, Emma, loved lavender, while another of my sisters, Helen, adored a dark, rich blue; and those colors were lovely, of course. But the crimson-colored rose was the one color I loved. I had a secret wish that someday, when a young man wished to marry me and make me his bride, he would give me a garnet as an engagement ring. The garnet was the same deep crimson as the rose.

"Violet! Violet!" I heard someone calling my name.

Leaning out of my window, I waved to Mr. O' Neale, the blacksmith. He was grinning up at me and smiling.

"And a top o' the mornin' to ye, lass! Mind ye dinna fall and break your neck, leanin' out o' that there window!"

Violets Are Blue

Mr. O' Neale was Irish and an immigrant like my family. I always felt a special kinship between us, for he had once admitted to missing his homeland. But I had never seen the blacksmith melancholy for a day. He was a cheerful man with a great, booming voice that could be heard even down by the harbor where the ships came in, bringing with them more immigrants from new lands who, like us, wished to make a new start.

"A top o' the mornin' to you too, Mr. O' Neale!" I shouted out the window, imitating his Irish accent.

He beamed up at me, waved once more, then went back to sweeping the street in front of his forge.

I sighed as I withdrew my head from outside and shut the window with a soft *thump*. I still held the rose in my hand, and the thorns were starting to prick my palm. Placing the flower in my hair, I walked over to the small mirror hanging from the wall to inspect how it looked. Satisfied, I turned to get dressed.

Mum had laid my blouse, skirt, and petticoats out on the end of my bed. Leaning over, I brushed the worn hem of my skirt with my fingertips. I longed for a beautiful, silky gown, with a high waist and a Japanese-

38

style sash, but I knew that could not be helped. Only wealthy ladies could afford such finery. I did own one treasure, and that was a dark red hair ribbon made of fine silk. It had been my late grandmother's, and Mum had given it to me for my fourteenth birthday.

I deftly braided my curls into a braid that reached to my waist, then tied the ribbon at the end to keep the braid secure. Emma was at the other end of our small room, helping little Grace into her frock. Robert and Henry were just waking up in their bed on the other side of the small room, wiping the sleep from their eyes. Mum smiled at me from the doorway, a soft "good morning" on her lips.

When Emma had finished braiding Grace's fair hair and we were dressed, we all sat down in the kitchen for breakfast. Besides being a kitchen, the room also acted as a dining room and a parlor. The apartment contained only three small rooms.

Father bowed his head in prayer, and all of us children followed him. *"Dear Lord,"* he prayed. *"May we honor You in all that we do today. Thank you for giving us all a restful sleep last night. May You bless this food to our bodies. In Your Name, Amen."*

"Violet, you look a bit weary, dear. Did you rest well last night?" Mum's brow furrowed with concern.

My answer was light. "Yes, Mum, I am fine. You needn't worry."

But she did not look convinced. Her eyes probed the deep purple circles under my eyes, a clear sign of a sleepless night. I pretended to be fine, and her brow finally smoothed.

"Father," Robert began. "Do you think you could take us to the harbor today? I love to see the ships coming and going."

"I'm sorry, son, but I have work to do today. My carpentry work is in full demand and I cannot afford to lose a day." Father's voice was regretful, but stern. Robby's face dropped in disappointment.

"But..." and at this Robby looked up with hope in his eyes, "you may be hearing quite a lot about ships in the next few weeks."

"Why, Father?" I asked.

"I have read in the newspapers that there is a grand ship being built in Belfast, in Ireland. I do not know her name, but she is being built for size."

Robert's eyes gleamed. "Oh Father, to think what it would be like to sail on such a ship!"

"It is an honor you will have to do without, son. As you can see, we have no need of traveling by ship, nor the means for such an expensive voyage."

"I *long* to travel on such a ship! Such an *adventure!*" Helen said dramatically.

"Helen, you just spit bread crumbs in my face." With a rueful smile, Emma wiped her cheek with her napkin. "Take better care next time."

"Oh, I beg your pardon, Emma," Helen said, ducking her head. "But the honor of being on *such a ship*..." And just like that, Helen was off again, rapturously exclaiming over how grand it must be to cross the ocean, little remembering that we had done so just a few months ago. When Anna pointed this out to her twin, Helen nodded her head lightly, but continued on. I saw Henry roll his eyes, and Father was grinning.

"You have always been quite the talkative child, Helen," he said, pretending to be stern. "I do think it would be best if you attempted to control that habit of yours..."

"Father..." Helen said, knowing at once that he was teasing her.

"This does bring up an excellent point though, Helen," Mum began. "It is not at all proper for a child of your age to talk so much. Do you want to be thought improper?"

"No, Mum." Helen sighed, as if this was the answer expected of her and not her real belief.

"Then I would advise you to curb your tongue a bit more, child. Are you done eating?"

Helen nodded.

"Then you may go do your morning chores. All of you are free to go."

I watched my siblings leave the room. "Mum," I began. "Today is my day to make the bread."

"Yes, yes, of course, Violet. I set it to rise last night. Knead the dough and then it needs to rise for an hour more."

"I know, Mum," I said, smiling at her. "I have made the bread for many years. And you have taught me well."

She stroked my cheek. "I know you've been sad, dear." I started to protest, but she held up her hand as if to stop me and continued:

"And I think I know the reason why. Violet, nothing can replace our home. Never will I forget how you took your first steps right in that house in Eastbourne. It breaks my heart just as much as it breaks yours to have to leave."

"But Mum, how can we live here? How can we ignore all that we left behind?" My voice shook, and tears came to my eyes.

"I am not asking you to ignore it. Rather, I want you to remember it. Remember the happy times we had in Eastbourne. Never forget those, Violet."

"But, Mum, how am I to live without it?"

"Violet, Eastbourne is just a place. The secret to our house there feeling like *home* was our love for one another. I think... I think that you are refusing to love New York as well."

"Mum, how could you say that?"

"Listen to my words, dear. I think that you are refusing to let yourself love our new home here because you are worried about forgetting Eastbourne."

I paused. Mum was entirely correct. That was the reason I had been so miserable. In my fear of forgetting my old home, I had unconsciously held myself back from growing attached to this home as well. Thinking of our home in Eastbourne made the tears spill out of my eyes and down my cheeks.

"How did you know?" I asked, attempting to keep my voice steady.

"Because I experienced the same exact thing, Violet. Do you think I am less emotional only because I hide it for the sake of the children?"

I pondered that, for that was exactly what I *had* thought.

"It would never do for them to be discontent. And so, I attempted to keep my emotions controlled. I hid the fact that my heart was despairing over leaving the home I came to as a new wife. You can do the same.

The least we can do is show our gratitude towards your father for taking us to this new land."

I marveled at Mum's courage. If she could be so unselfish, the least I could do was control my emotions.

Father surprised me by saying at the breakfast table a few days later, "Violet, you are to work in the clothing factory soon. You start on the first of next week."

My spoon paused in midair. I saw Emma glance wildly at Mum in shock, and both the twins looked solemn. Choking to swallow the bite of food in my mouth, I asked Father, "But, why?"

Glancing mournfully across the table at me, he spoke in a melancholy voice:

"Violet, we do not have enough money to support this family with only me working. Your mother will be going with you, and Emma will be minding the children each day. Your mum and I have talked about this very carefully, child," he said. "And we have no other choice if we are to survive."

My breath seemed to be caught in my throat. Under the table, Emma squeezed my hand. A single tear glistened in her deep brown eyes. I saw my face mirrored in hers, and I knew I wore the same expression she did: shocked, confused, and most of all, scared. I remembered the frightening stories we had heard on the ship traveling here; how immigrants were treated terribly in factories; how they earned very little money; how they had to work in heat that was very intense for twelve hours each day, every day except Sunday. I had thought that life in America was bad, and here was something that was destined to make it worse. Fear clutched at my heart, threatening to overpower me.

Mum glanced at me with regret in her face. I could see her taking in my frozen face, my mouth hanging open, and the fear in my eyes. I saw her shake her head softly, as if to remind me to control my emotions. But this was just too much...

"How can you send me away? How can I *leave?* Do you expect me to go among strangers all alone? How

46

can I do that?" My words burst from my lips, surprising me with their fury. But then I went too far: "It's bad enough that I had to leave Eastbourne. Are you going to force me to leave everything I know?"

And with that I whirled from the table and flung myself onto my bed in my room. Hot tears of anger and sadness spilled down my cheeks and wet my pillow. At this moment I desired nothing more than to be at my old home in Eastbourne, far, far away from this strange, new, and uncertain land.

When I had cried all my tears, I took a piece of paper and a pen from my drawer. As I often did when I missed Eastbourne, I wrote a letter to Lillian:

Dear Lillian,

No, no, no, no, no!

Father has decided to send Mum and me to work at the clothing factory. The clothing factory, Lilli! I've heard horrible tales of people being mistreated in these horrible places. How can Father expect me to go work in that environment? I cannot think how I shall bear this.

Love,

Vi

CHAPTER 5

I awoke one morning to Mum shaking my shoulder gently.

"Violet, dear, it is time to get up," she whispered in my ear.

I opened my eyes halfway. The room was still very dark, for it was only five o' clock. I tried to roll over, but Mum prodded my shoulder harder. "Violet, you *must* get up, dear. We need to leave for the factory soon."

That made me sit up with a start. Reality hit me; this was the day that I had been dreading: the day that I would start work at the factory. My fears of this approaching day had grown and intensified by the hour, and I was now completely and utterly terrified. But of course I could not tell Mum that.

Yanking on my clothes, I followed Mum out the door, walking lightly so that I wouldn't awaken my sisters. The sky was a dark grey and hung with foreboding clouds. I shivered in my thin gown, wishing I had remembered to bring my shawl, for it was an extremely brisk September morning.

A few leaves floated down from the trees, landing in my hair. I plucked them out of my curls and placed them in my pocket. I would press them and send them to Lilli in my next letter. I kept my head down from then on, relying only on Mum's hand on my arm to guide my steps. It wasn't until she stopped that I, too, came to a stumbled halt.

Towering in front of us, stiff and foreboding, was the factory.

The door opened roughly at Mum's knock.

"Yes?" a grisly-looking man asked sullenly.

"I am here with my daughter to apply for a job."

"Right this way," he muttered. Mum and I fell into step behind him.

The factory was dark and noisy. I could hear machines rumbling behind doors, and the smells were dreadful.

"Sit here," our guide said, motioning towards two small wooden chairs in a messy office room. I sat down stiffly, and Mum followed.

"Now," the man began, after introducing himself as Mr. Woods, "would ya please let me know yer names?"

Mum quickly introduced us, but she barely had the words out of her mouth before Mr. Woods interrupted.

"Now, now, we don't normally accept new workers this late... I'm not so sure if we can..."

"Oh, let the kind lady and her daughter work, Frank," a stout woman said from the door. She introduced herself briefly as Mrs. Woods, Mr. Woods' wife. "Ya can't jist let 'em starve, can ya?"

Mum smiled gratefully at the lady, but I wasn't sure she had done us such a huge favor. I, for one, would have been satisfied to go home immediately. But

Mum was determined, and so I bit my tongue to keep from talking.

"Yer daughter," Mr. Woods began gruffly. "How old might she be?"

"Fourteen, sir," I answered in a whisper.

"Speak up, girl, I can hardly hear what ye're sayin'"

"I am fourteen, sir," I very nearly shouted.

"She's got spunk, jist like our Nellie," Mrs. Woods said approvingly, with a small smile on her face.

"Yes... I suppose she will do," Mr. Woods admitted. "Now what about you, ma'am? Do you have a history of fainting over dust or being weak-hearted?"

"I will do my best, sir," Mum said politely.

"Then you will do as well. You can both go and start now. My wife will show you ladies how." And with that, he stomped out of the room.

"Don't mind Frank," Mrs. Woods said kindly. "You'll get used to him in yer own good time. But, let's not tarry. Time's a' wastin', as I always say. We'd best get both of ya comfortable with the machines so that ye can git workin' jist as soon as possible."

52

Mum and I followed Mrs. Woods into one of the dark, steamy rooms. Now that we were right next to the noisy machines, the humming was loud enough to make my ears ring. I wondered how I was going to be able to stand this each day.

As if she could hear my question, Mrs. Woods turned and said, "You'll get used to the noise after a time. Most of them there youngsters put little bits o' cotton is their ears, to plug the noise."

At the word 'youngsters,' I started and stared in shock at the workers who were controlling the machines. There were some as young as five years old. It made me think of Grace working in this awful place, and I shuddered at the thought.

"Now then, it's pretty simple. Just push these strips of fabric through the machine, keepin' time with the treadle down there"—she pointed at a small treadle on the floor—"and mind ya don't go too fast. That'll cause bumps and ridges. Ya know how to use the sewin' machine, I presume?"

"I... I'm sure we will do fine," Mum said, although her voice betrayed her doubt. "Thank you so much for all your help, Mrs. Woods."

"It was my pleasure. Pay's six dollar a week, and you'll work every day except Sunday."

"Six dollars?" Mum asked in shock. "I was sure we'd get paid more."

"Sorry, ma'am," Mrs. Woods said apologetically. "That's the rule."

I watched her retreating figure as it left the room. Then, swallowing my fears, I turned and faced the machine and began to sew.

Sewing grew very tiresome after a fashion. The fabric blurred before my eyes after staring at it for hours on end. I grew tired and weary in no time, and yet I still had to keep working.

As I worked, I remembered our voyage on the ship that took us to America. In steerage, the conditions were terrible. Rats ate our little food, mice left holes in our blankets, and seawater stained everything. The smells below deck were sour and stale. I had spent all the time that I could on the deck, but the weather had been fearsome. At the time, I could not wait to get off that ship.

Thinking of ships made me think of the new one being built in Belfast. It was done by now, and she had a name: *Titanic.* Even the name reminds one of her sheer size and luxury. She was to be eight hundred and eighty-two feet and nine inches long, ninety-two feet and six inches wide, and to have a weight of fifty-two thousand and three hundred and ten tons. I gasped just thinking about it, and several little faces turned curiously in my direction.

Mum shook her head as if to say, *"Get back to work!"*

I bent once more over the machine, which, while I had been idling, was beginning to bunch up in a knot of thread. Gritting my teeth together, I began to slowly remove the extra stitches.

I had never seen the clock move so slowly; never had I wished more for the day to end. After what seemed like a year, it was time to leave.

"Oh, Mum, it was terrible!" I complained on our walk home.

"Perhaps we do not work in the most *desirable* of conditions..."

"Desirable?!" I sputtered. "They are positively dreadful!"

"... but we must do what we can to help the family survive!" Mum said sternly.

I ducked my head, blushing.

"Violet..." Mum said, stroking my hair. "I do not want you to speak a word of your complaints to anyone, and most importantly, *not* to your father. He already feels terrible that you have to work, but what can we do?"

I agreed. And so, when we arrived home, I gave cheerful reports, cutting out the loud noises, rotten smells, and steamy, sweltering heat.

As soon as I could escape the comfortable room, I went to my bedroom, where I pulled out a piece of

56

paper, my pen, and my ink. I lay across my bed and began to write to Lillian...

Oh, Lilli, it was terrible, just as I had suspected, I wrote. *I had to work in this horrid, noisy room that smelled awful and was far too warm for comfort. The work is wearisome, the man who runs the factory is a grouch, and I wish I could just refuse to have anything to do with the place. But I can't. I have to go back tomorrow, and the day after that, and the day after that, and on and on until Sunday. Then I have to work once more on Monday!*

I miss you so much, Lilli. How is it in Eastbourne? Do send me a long letter and describe everything. I'll feel as though I was there.

Love,

Violet

When my letter was complete, I folded it and placed it in an envelope addressed to Lilli's home in Eastbourne.

Sometime about two or three weeks after Mum and I first began working in the factory, something strange happened. I was working—and daydreaming—when all of a sudden I heard Mum coughing tremendously. I had heard her clear her throat before, but this was much worse. I ran to her side immediately.

"Mum, what is it?" I asked in alarm.

"Just a bit of dust, dear," she said calmly, attempting to stop coughing. "I'll be fine—you needn't be alarmed."

"Mum, maybe you should go home... Remember what Mr. Woods said."

"I'll be fine, dear, as I said. Besides, I'm not going to leave the job that I am being paid to complete, no matter how much dust there is."

I could not convince her otherwise, much as I did try. Finally, I reluctantly returned to my sewing machine, for she would not be moved. But the air was filled with dust and the heat was penetrating. I heard Mum coughing several times more during the hour, each one growing in turn.

By now, I was beginning to be alarmed. I begged and pleaded with Mum, but she would not leave. I offered to ask Mrs. Woods if Mum could have a break, but my mother refused.

"No Violet, I do not need to stop working," she insisted. Her face was pale, and her body shook as another set of coughs came on. "You see," she said when she could speak once more, "I am fine."

I was fully and completely aware that Mum was *not* fine, but I knew I must respect her wishes. It was not until she very nearly fainted an hour later that she finally permitted me to talk with Mrs. Woods about Mum leaving early.

Leaning on my arm, Mum walked slowly outside, and then took a deep breath slowly.

"Mum," I said firmly. "You *must* go home."

"Yes, yes, I will, Violet," she said vaguely. "But I will be back tomorrow. And you'd best not try to convince me otherwise, for I stand firm."

She was silent for a while as I walked her home, slowly.

"Violet?" Mum said softly, ten minutes later.

"Yes, Mum?" I asked questioningly.

"I... I know and you know that I cannot work in that factory. But I don't want you talking about it, especially not in front of Mr. Woods. He would only be too happy to fire me and have one less worker to pay. I do not want to appear weak. We need the money, Violet," she added urgently. "Do you understand?"

"Yes, Mum, I do. But... can I ask you a question?"

"Of course, dear."

"Why does Father suddenly need money? We have been in America for quite a few months, and only now does he need extra income? Why did he not ask us to work when we first arrived here?" Blushing, I realized I may have said too much. "That is... if you don't mind answering."

"I don't, dearest. Your father..." she sighed. "Your father is trying to earn extra money so that we can help William and Amelia come here, to America."

I gasped. William and Amelia were Lilli's parents! Lilli was going to come to New York!

Mum glanced at my happy smile and her own face stretched into a smile. "I know how you miss your friend. I miss Amelia, too. And William and your Papa have been good friends for many a year. We will all be happy to have the whole family here."

I smiled at Mum, and helped her walk home. Suddenly, my future looked a whole lot brighter.

CHAPTER 6

"Grace, *please!* Hold your head steady!" I complained as I tried to stop my littlest sister from falling headfirst into the soapy water. Grace was a squirmy little girl, and she refused to hold still for very long periods of time. "You know Mum wants me to get your hair good and clean. Please hold still!" I insisted, as she made another attempt to squirm from my arms.

"Sorry," Grace mumbled. But soon a soap bubble caught her eye, and she reached her little fingers up to pop it. The bubble floated away, and Grace lost her balance. With a *splash!* she fell into the tub.

"Grace..." I said in a scolding tone. "What will Mum say? She told me to only wash your hair. Her exact words were..."

"*Don't get wet!*" Mum recited from the doorway, interrupting me. She turned to Grace, who was pouting. "Mind your sister next time."

"Yes, ma'am," Grace sighed.

I had turned to finish scrubbing Grace's curls when Anna skidded into the room, catching her breath.

"Violet... I was down at the post office with Helen, and..."

Mum interrupted, "Anna, you know you shouldn't be out of the apartment on your own..."

"I know, Mum, I wasn't..." she paused to take a breath. "I was with Helen... and with Robby... and Father had told us to... to..."

"Anna, what is it?" I asked impatiently.

"There... there was a letter for you, Vi. It came in the mail. Here," she said, handing me a thick envelope.

I snatched the letter eagerly, my soapy hands leaving water marks on the envelope. "Mum, may I?"

"Yes, Violet, you can go. I am sure you will want to read Lilli's letter in private." Mum smiled indulgently. "I will finish with Grace."

I smiled gratefully at Mum, than flew out of the room and into the bedroom. I tore open the envelope with eager fingers, my eyes scanning the page.

Dearest Violet,

What news, what wonderful news I have for you! Father is making arrangements for us to come to America, to New York soon! Is that not wonderful? I will see you! We will be neighbors. No longer apart, we will be rejoined once more. Oh, how hard it is for me to wait for that day when I can talk to you in person as we used to do in Eastbourne. Father has only to earn enough to pay for our fare across the ocean, and then we shall be off!

Your request for a long letter must be, sadly, ignored, for I can write nothing else... at least for now. The reason for this is that Father is calling for me. He is to walk me to the post, where I shall mail this.

I hope that we may be together as soon as possible, dear friend. Until then, I remain,

Your best friend always,

Lillian

Oh! I knew this already, but that did not make it any less wonderful. To hear Lilli herself confirm that yes, she was coming to America, sent a thrill through me. I almost wished she were coming to New York on the *Titanic*, but of course that was not possible. It must cost a fortune for just a third class ticket.

"Violet! It's your turn to wash your hair!" Emma called.

I couldn't wash my hair. I couldn't sit, or be still or anything else that required primitive motion. Not now. Not for awhile. I was too jittery and excited. I had to run, I had to *move*.

No, I had to wash my hair.

Emma's head popped in through the open doorway to confirm this. "Violet," she said in a motherly tone. "Mum insists that you come *now*."

"I will, I *will*, Emma! Give me just one minute."

I snatched another piece of paper and my quill. Then I quickly scribbled a reply to Lillian:

I am elated to hear your news, Lilli. It fills me with the greatest joy, more joy than I could ever imagine. Just think—to be neighbors! I am hoping that my work at the clothing factory will help get you here faster, sooner. If it weren't for you, I feel as though I would put my foot down and refuse to work at that dreadful place. But it is for you, so I shall work, gladly. If it will help to bring you to America, Lilli, I will do anything.

With that, I sealed my letter and wrote Lillian's address on the front. I had to get this to the post office before it closed.

Mum was waiting for me when I returned from the post. "Violet, was it necessary that you send your reply right this minute?" she asked me.

"No, I suppose it was not *necessary*," I admitted. "But I was eager for her to get my reply as soon as possible."

Mum smiled a small smile, as though recalling a private joke. She helped me gently remove my gown so that I was only wearing my chemise and stockings. "Kneel over the bucket," she directed. Then Mum poured warm water over my hair, and then lathered my curls with soap.

"Mum?" I asked.

"Yes?"

"Are you sure you are fine? At the factory," I explained.

"Violet," Mum sighed. "We have gone over this many times. I am not leaving that factory until Mr. Woods *kicks* me out. Do you understand? I don't want you to mention this again." She paused to stroke my brow. "I am fine, dear. Really. No need to worry."

I nodded my head, but my mind was anything but reassured. I had seen Mum working at the factory. She was always extremely tired when she came home, and she almost fainted while working in that heat. I knew my bothering her about quitting was making it worse, but I couldn't help it—I was worried for her. I didn't want to lose my dear mother, even if it meant Lilli couldn't come to America.

I suddenly turned around and gave Mum a big squeeze, soap in my hair and all.

"Why did you do that, dear?" she asked in surprise, hugging me back.

"Because I love you," I answered. "And Mum," I added, two tears trembling in my eyes. "I don't want to lose you."

"Oh Violet," Mum said, gently ducking my head into the tub to rinse my hair. "I have no intention of leaving any time soon."

Hearing the strength and assurance in her voice, I was finally reassured and tried to think of happier things.

The next day I went to the butcher's shop to buy some meat. To my surprise, the butcher, Mr. Peterson, was not there. In his place was a young man who looked to be about sixteen. I bought the meat and was turning to leave when the young man tapped my shoulder.

"You would be Miss Bradshaw, correct?" he asked.

I whirled quickly. "Sir, how do you know my name?"

"My uncle has told me all about you. He says you come every Wednesday to buy a pound of meat, normally whatever we have on sale. Is that true?"

"I don't know why that would be any of your business, sir. And who might your uncle be?"

"I'm not 'sir,' I'm Ethan. And my uncle's the butcher. Pleased to make your acquaintance, Miss Bradshaw." He held out is hand in a friendly gesture.

I dropped a curtsy. "And I'm not 'Miss Bradshaw'—I'm just Violet."

69

He grinned, then gestured toward my basket. "Is that enough to feed your family? I was sure that there were nine of you."

"We get along well enough," I said stubbornly, blushing.

"Now, I didn't mean to offend you, Violet," Ethan said quickly. "It just didn't seem like much meat to be taking home to a large family."

"It's all we can afford," I said softly. I curtsied once more, than left the shop.

CHAPTER 7

I trudged home from my shift at the factory, my shoulders drooping. Mrs. Woods had been absent today, and without his wife to pacify him, Mr. Woods had been especially disagreeable. He had deducted five cents from my pay for pausing in my work.

"Don't let it happen again!" he had shouted angrily.

And though I wanted to shout back in an angry tone that matched his, I simply had to bite my tongue and go back to my work. It was very trying.

So wound up in my own thoughts was I that I barely heard the soft mewing coming from under the apartment stairs. Bending down, I noticed a small kitten. His eyes were not yet open; he must have been only a few days old.

There was clearly only one thing to be done. I bent, and pulling a handkerchief from my pocket, I scooped the little kitten up in my hand. He was barely the size of my

palm. Then I turned and climbed the rest of the way up the dark, rank staircase, to our apartment.

"You'll never guess what I..." I started to say, as I opened the door.

"Violet!" I heard Anna say in annoyance. "I just scrubbed the floor! Look where you're going!"

"Oops! Sorry, Anna," I apologized.

"Where's Mum?" Emma asked curiously, entering the room.

"She decided to stay an extra shift at the factory," I answered. "She was hoping to make more money to bring home to Father."

"All the better," Emma said.

I turned towards her, confused. "Why did you say "all the better" like that?"

"We're trying to get the fall cleaning done before Mum comes home," she whispered.

"It'll be a grand surprise!" Anna said, joining in.

72

"*I* sure hope it's grand," Helen commented sourly, coming through the door. She was heaving a heavy mattress outside to air. "Emma's making me do all the hard work! It's not *fair.*"

"Where are the boys?" I questioned Emma.

"They went to help Father with one of his carpentry jobs. He said he might put them to work." She winked at me.

"Ah..." I said, understanding.

"Well, I don't see how it's fair for them to leave *us* with all the work!" Helen complained.

"Oh Helen," I said. "You shouldn't complain like that."

"I don't care!" she said in a contrary tone. "If I want to complain, I will!"

Anna stopped the argument midway.

"Violet," she said. "What's that in your hand?"

Through all the commotion, I had forgotten about the kitten.

"I found him under the steps," I said.

"Here, hand him to me," Emma said, holding out her hand.

I gave her the kitten, and she nuzzled the top of his head with her finger.

"Oh, how sweet," Anna cooed.

"What should we name him?" Helen asked eagerly.

All of a sudden the room erupted in a chorus of suggestions.

"Stop!" Emma ordered. "Now, since Violet found the kitten, I think she should name him."

"Well..." I said. "We should name him something that reminds us of him."

"How?" Anna asked.

"He's gray, with white spots," I said. "Perhaps something along the lines of..."

"A kitten!" Grace exclaimed, running into the room.

"Yes," I said. "We're thinking of what to name him, Grace. Do you have an idea?"

"Um..." Grace said slowly, scratching her head in a comical manner. "I think we should name him..."

Before she could get the words out of her mouth, the little kitten leapt from Emma's hands and jumped onto the table, knocking over a bottle of milk in the process. Emma looked at me in horror, but the littlest girls were giggling. The kitten—shrieking at finding himself soaked—stretched his claws out, digging his nails into the table. But the only thing he managed to do was slip in the pool of milk and drench himself further. Helen, Anna, and Grace exploded into uproarious laughter.

"Here," I said, picking up the dripping kitten and handing it to Grace. "Name him quickly before something else happens."

"Milky," Grace said decidedly.

Minutes later, we were all cleaning as though our life depended on it. Emma had been polishing the silver when I had first arrived, and she sat to finish her uncompleted task. Helen grudgingly pulled the rest of the mattresses outside onto the fire escape, where they could air, and then set to dusting. Anna was amusing

Grace, and although it looked as though she was doing nothing, it was a huge help to us workers.

I had been cleaning up the milk that the kitten had spilled—re-washing the floor in the process—for quite some time when I heard footsteps. I jumped, startled, and then relaxed.

"Oh, it's just you, Helen," I said in relief.

"Violet..." Helen said slowly. "Do you ever miss Eastbourne?"

It took me a minute to collect my scattered thoughts. "What?" I asked in confusion.

"Eastbourne," Helen said. "Don't you ever miss it?"

She stood and walked toward me, then dropped into my lap. I stroked her hair.

"Of course I do, dear," I said gently. "But why this sudden change? I thought no one could be happier to be here in America than you."

"Of course no one was happier. Or rather, no one *pretended* to be happier."

Her statement only managed to confuse me further.

76

"Helen, I want you to tell me right now, without any excuses: *what is wrong?*"

She glanced up at me with sadness in her brown eyes. "Do you have to ask?" I saw a tear drip out of her eye; it left a wet spot on my dirty apron.

It was then that I experienced a sudden revelation. Helen missed Eastbourne just as much as I did, just as much as Mum. *Her* way of hiding it was doing the opposite of her emotions: pretending she could not be happier to be in New York, hiding the fact that she was no less broken-hearted then I was.

I could not be more wrong in my opinion of her.

And, having experienced the same emotions she was speaking of now, I knew that it was best not to say a word. Instead, I continued to stoke her hair silently, neither of us speaking.

That afternoon was the first time I actually understood my dramatic little sister.

"She's coming! She's coming!" Anna called frantically. She and Grace were positioned at the window, poised to alert the rest of us the minute Mum was spotted.

"Quick, hide! Violet, put that broom in the corner! Helen, pick up that rag! And quiet, quiet, don't ruin the surprise!"

I smiled at Emma's fiercely-whispered orders, but I obeyed, making sure everything was perfect.

"She's walking up the step! She's turning the handle of the door... oh, now she's coming inside! I hear her footsteps; Grace, is it *so* hard to stay quiet?"

Anna continued to give reports until Emma whispered:

"Anna, quiet! Mum will hear you!"

We all jumped when we heard Mum's knock on the door. Emma rushed to open it.

"Well, girls, how was your day?" Mum asked. Her voice sounded weary.

Suddenly, she looked around, confused.

"Emma," Mum said. "Where are your sisters?"

"Well... you see..." Emma said, stalling for time.

This was our cue! I motioned with my hand to Anna, Helen, and Grace and we all jumped out from under the kitchen table.

"Surprise!"

"We cleaned the house for you, Mum! All the fall cleaning is finished!" Helen said proudly.

"Finished?" Mum asked in disbelief.

We all nodded eagerly, grinning.

"Oh, girls..." Mum said, a smile spreading over her tired face. "Thank you."

Then she opened her arms, and we all ran to hug her.

Emma had set the water to boil on the stove for Mum's tea, and it was now ready. I took one of our few china cups from the cupboard, put a precious teaspoon of honey into the bottom of the cup, and then poured tea over the top. Helen handed me a spoon from the cupboard. Mum was soon sitting at the table, sipping her tea.

We were all chatting together in a cheerful manner when suddenly Mum looked up, as though she had forgotten something. Then she smiled in a secretive manner.

"Emma, go look on the top shelf of that cupboard."

Emma went, and returned with a metal tin. She shook it lightly, and I heard something rattling around inside.

"Emma, don't break them! Now hand it to me, please," Mum said.

We all gathered around, wondering what was in the tin. Mum lifted the lid, and we all leaned over her...

Nestled in a clean napkin were over a dozen ginger biscuits!

"Here," Mum said, handing each of us a biscuit. "I thought you girls deserved a treat. And after this lovely surprise, I *know* you do."

"But, Mum, ginger biscuits are..."

"... just what we can afford right now," Mum answered. "So you needn't worry, Emma."

The sweet biscuits had a delicious bite to them, and I ate mine slowly, savoring this rare treat.

"But, wait," I said. "Where are Father and the boys?"

"Oh, they came home hours ago," Anna answered. "Didn't you notice?"

I realized that I had been so busy cleaning that I *hadn't* noticed.

"But how could you not know that?" Emma questioned. "Father doesn't like to stay out working past dark. If he can't finish a job by sunset, he comes back in the morning to finish it. Sunset was hours ago.

"Then what time is it now?" I asked in surprise.

"It's ten o' clock exactly," Mum said. "You girls *have* had a long day. We should all go to bed."

I helped Emma clean up the crumbs, and then we all went to our beds. Grace especially must have been very tired, for I found her lying on her bed five minutes later, still in her clothes, sound asleep. I gently pulled her nightgown over her head and tucked her in.

Emma was already asleep in the bed we shared, and I quickly ran a brush through my hair before joining her. Sliding between the sheets, I leaned over and blew out our candle for the night.

CHAPTER 8

"Do you call that *neatly* stitched?!"

I winced, looking up at Mr. Woods, who was towering over me, his angry frame shaking.

"Well?" He was clearly still waiting for an answer.

"Yes, I do call that neatly stitched, sir," I said softly.

"Well, I call it loose and sloppy work! Impudent girl!" He raised his hand in the air, and slapped me across the face. "There, take that for your smart talk!"

Anger boiled inside of me at this unjust punishment, and it was all I could do to control it. I felt tears coming to my eyes, and I fought to hold them back. My cheek stung dreadfully where he had slapped me.

Mr. Woods was still shouting:

"And if I *ever* have to correct your mistakes again, mark my words, it *will* come out of yer pay!"

This was too dreadful. I ducked my head over my sewing, mumbling my apologies.

"I can't hear ya, girl! Speak up!"

I whispered, this time a bit louder, "My apologies, sir."

I sighed when he finally left the room. His weekly visits were always terrible. I had seen him slap the face of a young girl last week, who looked to be but sixteen years of age.

"He's a vile man!" I said suddenly.

Heads whipped around and stared at me as though I had gone insane. As a rule, you don't ever criticize Mr. Woods—*ever.* It just isn't done.

"Shh!" one girl whispered fiercely. I noticed that she was the same girl who had been slapped last week, a pretty Irish girl with a long braid of curly auburn hair. "He'll hear ye!"

"I don't care if he does! He is rude and cruel to all of us!" My little outburst startled even me.

"But he'll fire ye! Do ye want to be cold and hungry in the streets?"

That silenced me.

Mum worked late again that night, and once more, I came home alone. Emma was always cheerful when I arrived, and she would willingly tell me all that had happened that day. I would reply vaguely. More often then not, I would go to bed quickly after I had eaten the dinner that Emma kept warm for me. Father would be home, and he would help Emma put the children to bed. None of us would ever see Mum come home at night, for she arrived well around twelve o' clock.

But tonight, I was determined to wait up for her. Wrapping myself in a warm shawl, I sat by the window, keeping a weary vigil for Mum.

The hours grew late. I yawned, thinking how nice it would be to climb into bed and go to sleep. But I couldn't—I must stay up for Mum.

To keep myself awake, I began to think on all that had happened in the one month since Mum and I had started working at the factory. The first two weeks

84

were easy—Mrs. Woods let us come home early, for Mum's sake. But now that Mrs. Woods was gone—and I didn't know to *where* she had gone—Mr. Woods had started to lay down the law. Late hours, harder work— nothing seemed too cruel for him.

My eyelids grew heavy, and drooped slowly, almost closing. I fought to keep them open.

The wind whistled around the house eerily. I wondered what could be taking Mum so long to get home. In the kitchen, a single candle was still burning. I tiptoed into the quiet room, wondering who could be awake at this late hour.

It was Father.

His eyebrows raised in alarm at my entrance. "Violet, are you ill?"

"No, Father," I said quickly. "I have been waiting for Mum to come home."

I expected him to tell me that it was too late for me to be awake, and then to order me back to my bed.

But he didn't. Instead, he motioned for me to come and sit with him at the table.

"I have been waiting for her as well," he whispered. "Perhaps you can wait with me. But don't speak a word, for the others are asleep and it is nearly midnight."

I nodded my agreement, and then whispered questioningly, "Father?"

"Yes, Violet?" His deep voice was inquisitive.

"I'm worried..." I took a deep breath. "About Mum. She truly is not well, Father. I have seen her work in that horrid factory—I have *seen* her, Father. It's terrible, just terrible. She coughs and chokes and faints. And yet, she refuses to quit. Mr. Woods would be glad to have her removed from the group of workers, she says, and she does not intend to please him by quitting. And Mr. Woods is just so terrible, and..." I cut myself off quickly, realizing all of a sudden that I had disobeyed Mum and complained to Father about the factory.

"I know, Vi, I know." His voice was weary, like one whom has been called upon to explain something for the tenth time.

"Then why don't you tell her, Father? Tell her that she cannot harm herself by working in the..."

86

"I have *tried,* Violet! I have tried very hard. But your mother is determined. Nothing I say can change her mind."

We both jumped when we heard a knock at the door.

"That would be your mum," Father said. "You can go back to bed, Violet."

I wanted to stay, but I knew it was already very late.

"Yes, Father," I said, sighing. And then I turned and tiptoed back

I was walking home from the factory one evening, when I happened to stop at Mr. O' Neale's blacksmith forge. I was exhausted from the factory; every bone in my body ached.

"Hello, Violet!" Mr. O' Neale called out to me.

"Hello, Mr. O' Neale," I answered in a faint voice.

"Saints preserve us! What's wrong with ye, Vi? Yer lookin' a bit sick."

"Nothing is wrong with me, although I am tired. It's the factory," I said, as if that explained everything.

He nodded in a knowing fashion.

"I heard from yer little brother that you and yer mam were workin' there. Are ye at the clothing factory?"

I nodded.

"Aye, me old bones get to achin' just hearin' about it. That Mr. Woods is quite a gentleman, isna he?" His voice was sarcastic.

I nodded again—I simply didn't seem to have the energy to do more than that.

"Did he slap ye?" Mr. O' Neale asked inquisitively.

I blushed. I had forgotten about the scene earlier in the week, in which Mr. Woods had taken out his anger on my left cheek.

Suddenly, my vision started to blur.

That's strange, I thought, struggling to keep a grip on reality.

Elizabeth Rose

I heard Mr. O' Neale speaking, but I couldn't make out the words. My stomach twisted, my head felt faint, and the street seemed to spin under me. I wanted to hold onto something, but my blurry vision wouldn't allow me to locate anything for support. I felt my knees buckling.

"Violet!" Someone called my name from far away. I heard quick footsteps.

I was falling, falling, and I couldn't think why. Memories of the factory today made my head spin, and I began to feel more and more dizzy.

But I didn't hit the street, as I had expected. Instead, I seemed to rise above it, as though I was flying, cradled by strange arms I did not recognize. I heard Mr. O' Neale speaking again:

"Yer quick, lad! There, catch her before she hits her head! Steady now, dinna let her fall. Her apartment's just down the street.

Who was quick? Who was going to hit her head? After a few minutes had passed, I heard a door open, and then the creaking of stairs as someone walked up them.

Voices suddenly started calling my name, in varying tones of alarm. I felt someone, Emma perhaps, place a cool rag on my forehead.

"She's fainted. Get her to bed, quickly."

I recognized the voice, but I was unable to place it.

And then everything went black.

CHAPTER 9

I awoke to find that my head was extremely sore. I rubbed it, but that seemed only to worsen it. Blinking, I opened my eyes.

Why was I in bed? The clock on the wall read nine o' clock in the morning. I should have been at the factory hours ago.

"Violet?" a voice questioned. It was Emma.

"Emma?" I said. "Why—why am I in bed?"

"Because you fainted, dear."

Suddenly, it all started to come back to me.

"What—what happened, Emma?"

"You must have been dreadfully weary and tired after your shift at the factory. I don't know what happened, really," she admitted. "All of a sudden you were being carried up the stairs by Mr. Hartley, your body limp in his arms. I was a bit alarmed. But he—Mr.

Hartley—explained that you must be extremely tired from your work."

The name didn't register with my brain.

"Who is Mr. Hartley?" I asked in confusion.

"The butcher's nephew. Surely you've seen him before."

"Ethan." The name was not a question.

"You know him?"

"Yes, although I knew only his first name. He commented on how little meat we buy. He thought the portions were a bit small."

"They are. But it's all we can afford."

"That's what *I* said!"

We both laughed for a minute, then sighed. Soon after, Emma went back to the kitchen to complete some chores, and I fell into a deep, dreamless slumber.

The next time I awoke, it was evening. Dr. Baylor was leaning over me, listening to my heart.

"Hmm..." he said. "Hmm, indeed... hmm..."

I wish he would say more then just "hmm." It was beginning to bother me.

"Hmm..." he said once more. "Yes, Mrs. Bradshaw, you have done well. Rest is all she needs. By tomorrow morn, she shall be fit as a fiddle."

"Thank you, sir," Mum said gratefully.

"What exactly made you faint, miss?" The doctor's gray eyes peered over his wiry spectacles and seemed to bore into me.

"I... I don't know..." I said, struggling to remember. The images in my head were growing stronger, but they were still very faint. "I... I think I was overly-tired... from the factory."

"Ah, yes." He nodded his balding head. "Those factories are no good for people, especially the young ones." He shook is head sadly, then looked sternly at Mum. "I would advise you to keep your daughter out of the factories, ma'am. Out for *good*. That heat can do mighty bad things to children. Fainting's not the worst that could happen."

Mum protested that she had no other choice; her children would starve.

"I know what you mean, ma'am," Dr. Baylor said sympathetically. "Believe me, I do. But hear me out: that factory will do nothing but harm to your daughter. It'll do harm to you, too."

At that moment, Mum coughed, then excused herself from the room.

"Your mother," the doctor said. "Have you tried convincing her to stay away from those factories?"

"Yes, sir," I said miserably. "I have, but she's determined. She won't listen. We're trying to bring our friends over from England, sir," I explained. "Father's job doesn't earn enough money to do that. So Mum and I had to go to work.

"Emma minds the children each day," I continued. "Mum and I work at the factory from seven in the morning to seven in the evening. And she's been staying extra hours, to earn more.

"The boss is awfully mean, and he works us dreadfully hard. I'm not the only one who feels so. Everyone who works in that factory agrees that he's terribly cruel. But what can we do, sir?" In a despairing voice, I added: "We've no other choice."

94

The doctor said no more. He simply nodded his head, then left. I heard the door shut behind him as he exited the apartment building.

"Well, you will have to stay out of the factory, Vi," Mum said, after letting the doctor out. "At least, that is, until you have regained your strength."

"No!" I protested. "Mum, I cannot leave you in that dreadful place alone!"

"Violet," she said in a stern voice. "You say you cannot, but you will. You will obey me and not work in that factory for one week."

The days passed slowly, very slowly. I heard Mum leave each morning, but I was not allowed to await her arrival at night.

"Your health, dear," was all that Mum said.

My health indeed! I was in a much more desirable condition, especially after all this rest I had been getting. Mum should have been the one at home, resting and staying away from the factory. But there she was, braving the stench and heat—*for me*.

I couldn't bear to think of it that way.

I passed my time each day writing to Lillian:

Dearest Lilli,

Oh, it's been dreadful. I fainted on my way home from the factory one day, and Ethan—the butcher's apprentice and nephew—carried me to my apartment. Then the doctor came to see me, and he was forever saying "hmm..." and such, until I was nearly driven mad! When he finally stopped with his "hmm..."'s, he informed Mum that I would need to stay home for several days, resting. He didn't want me to go back to the factory for at least a week.

Mum will not ignore his orders. But neither will she allow us to starve. She insists on working at the factory, although it does terrible things to her. She refuses to listen to my protests. Am I supposed to sit around, just waiting for the factory to wear her out so much that she dies?

I can't think of anything more terrible than losing my Mum.

Love,

Violet

After signing my name, I sealed the letter in an envelope and addressed it. I felt a wave of worry come over me, for I was certain that if Mum were allowed to work at the factory for much longer, she would die. I raised a hand to my warm forehead, wondering if I was catching a fever.

Anna glanced at me from her position at the table, kneading the bread for supper.

"Vi, are you ill? Should I call Father?" Her voice heightened in alarm.

"No!" I said, in a fiercer voice then I intended.

She jumped a little and looked startled.

"No, Anna, I am fine," I added, this time much more gently.

She gave me a look that said, *You don't look fine.*

I ignored her, and turned my attention to Henry, who was on the floor, playing with a set of wooden blocks Father had made. Grace was sitting with him, and she was smiling happily up at him as he helped her build castles and towers.

I could not think of something to amuse myself. I felt so useless just sitting here like this.

"I'm leaving," I announced to Emma.

"Where to?" she asked lightly.

"Mum wouldn't like it," Anna added importantly.

"Oh, do be quiet, Anna!" I said impatiently.

"Violet, where *are* you going?" Emma asked me.

"To the factory. Mum needs help, and I'm not going to waste my time sitting here."

"You had better leave her alone, Vi. Don't you know that it only makes Mum feel worse when you pressure her to leave that factory? Now come help me with dinner." Emma's voice was not very persuasive, as if she doubted that I would leave.

"I am leaving, Emma, and nothing you say can stop me!"

I snatched my shawl on my way out the door. Emma's worried face spun around the corner.

"Violet, are you sure you feel well enough?"

I didn't answer her, but instead ran out into the street, slamming the door shut behind me.

Once outside, I began to have doubts. My head was feeling a bit dizzy, after all. Maybe it wasn't such a good idea...

"Violet! Are you well?"

I whirled at the sound of Ethan's voice.

"Yes, as a matter of fact, I am. I am perfectly fit."

"Violet, come on, don't be curt. You fainted barely three days ago."

"Why does my welfare concern you so much, *Mr.* Hartley? Why do you have to be like everyone else and question me so much? Can't anyone just leave me alone?!"

And with that, I burst into tears and ran down the sidewalk towards the factory, leaving a bewildered Ethan behind me.

I gasped as I ran, tears streaming down my face. I had no idea why I was crying. The tears had come on so suddenly, and before I knew it I was weeping for no apparent reason. I ordered myself to stop, but my weak orders were in vain.

The factory was not far away. Before long, it was right in front of me. I stopped abruptly, swinging open the heavy door, then ran in.

There, in the sweltering heat, sat Mum.

She was barely recognizable. Her cheeks were pale and worn. Her brow was damp with sweat. Her eyes were red and tired. She continued to push the fabric through the sewing machine tirelessly, though I could see her arms shaking with fatigue.

I watched in horror as Mr. Woods entered the room. He headed straight for Mum.

First came the usual tirade about neat stitches, although Mum did not answer back as saucily as had I.

Good, I thought. *He won't punish her. He'll see that she is eager to obey him.*

I was wrong.

With an angry bellow, Mr. Woods raised his hand. He whipped Mum across the face, and she fell to the floor weeping. Then he kicked her. She begged for mercy. He gave none, but instead, kicked her again.

I could barely stand watching this. Anger boiled up in me, and I wanted to dash into the room and kick him, but my feet seemed hammered to the floor.

With one last check around the room, stopping to slap my Irish friend for tangled thread, he left.

I sighed in relief, then almost gasped in horror. Mum's cheek was bruised and bloody. Her hands were scraped from the rough floor.

I shrieked, "Mum!"

Her head turned in shock. "Violet? What on earth are you doing here?"

CHAPTER 10

It was extremely difficult for me to open my mouth to answer Mum's question. Her words hung in the air, and I almost choked as I tried to answer them.

But I didn't get the chance.

Mum's face suddenly went ashen gray. Her eyes seemed to roll back into her head. And then—without any warning—she passed out and fell to the floor.

The room lost all control and seemed to swim with masses of people, all trying to help Mum in any way they could. The kind Irish girl was the only one who kept her head.

"Water!" she called. "I need water! And smelling salts—does anyone have smelling salts?"

A middle-aged woman walked forward, clutching a small bottle.

"Here," she said, pressing the smelling salts into my hand. "For your mother."

I wanted to thank her, but my lips were frozen. I just stood there, like a statue, until the Irish girl shook me.

"Miss!" she said urgently. "Miss, your mam needs you! Can you watch over her? I need to get me da. He'll carry her home."

I nodded my head, and attempted to move my feet. I felt stiff and cold, as though my body was now made of wood.

I gripped the Irish girl's arm before she could go.

"Thank you, thank you so much! What is your name?"

"Mary," the girl answered. "Mary O' Neale."

"Then your father is..."

"He's the blacksmith, miss. And I need to go get him now. Could you please let go of me arm?"

"What? Oh, oh, I'm so sorry, yes, of course!" I said all in a rush, letting go of her arm quickly.

"I'll run as fast as me legs can carry me! Don't worry," she added reassuringly. "Your mother will be fine."

I was not so sure.

I waited by Mum's side on the dirty factory floor. She was beginning to revive. I stared at her pale face in desperation. I had told her she was going to fall ill, and yet, she still worked. Would she continue to do her job at this factory until she died? I didn't want to think of that.

"Miss!" I heard Mary call.

I ran to her, my eyes pleading for some good news.

"I've got me da, miss," she said. "He'll carry her home. Come, miss."

Mr. O' Neale was leaning over Mum.

"Yes," he said. "She'll need a doctor. Too much dirt in her lungs. I'm afraid she's gonna be sick."

I ran to him. "What can I do?"

"Go home," he said. "Let Emma know what's happened. She's not to be alarmed. Then go get the doctor."

I ran home with urgency pounding in my steps. My legs seemed slow and heavy, weighing me down. For the first time in my life, I wished for the wings of a bird. Eventually, I reached the apartment.

Emma was alarmed but not surprised to hear about Mum's condition. She urged me to hurry on to the doctor's.

Dr. Baylor did not live far away. His apartment was in a building far nicer then ours', not too far down the street. I ran to his building, my sides heaving as I gasped for breath.

"Dr. Baylor! Dr. Baylor!" I banged on his door many a time, calling the doctor's name over and over.

"Dr. Baylor, please come!"

The door squeaked open a crack. A nervous maid was inside, holding a dishrag.

"I'm sorry, miss," she said. "The doctor's not here."

Not here? Then where *was* he?

"Thank you, ma'am. Might you tell me where he is?"

"He's got a patient, miss. He's down at the Woods'."

The Woods'?

"Do you mean the Mr. and Mrs. Woods who run the clothing factory?"

"That's them, miss. The missus is awful sick. He's been tendin' to her for near two hours."

"Which way?"

She pointed with the hand clutching the dishrag.

"Thank you!"

The maid nodded her head, then closed the door.

The Woods' house was in a newer district, cleaner then my neighborhood. Their apartment building had shiny-clean steps and window boxes. I grimaced up at them, but I bravely ran up the steps. Mum's health was all that mattered now.

I knocked on the door quickly. A maid with a lacy cap peaked around the door.

"Yes, miss?"

"I'd like to see the doctor."

"He's not available, miss. He's tending to Mrs. Woods."

Biting my tongue so as not to scream, I repeated, "I would like to see the doctor."

"I'm sorry, miss." She did not sound sorry. "You can't."

She started to close the door, but I pushed through quickly.

"Miss!" she said as I headed down the hall. "You're not allowed!"

I heard a tremendous coughing coming from one of the bedrooms. I opened the door slowly...

There, in a bed, lay Mrs. Woods.

But *was* she Mrs. Woods? She did not look at all like the cheerful and brisk lady I had met on my first day at the factory. Her face was pale and drawn, and her body was thin.

She looked up wearily as I came in.

"Jane?" she said, thinking I was the maid. "Is that you?"

"No, ma'am, it's me, Violet Bradshaw."

"Violet? What are you doing here child?"

108

"I need the doctor."

She glanced up at Dr. Baylor, who was packing his bag.

"I'm through with you, Mrs. Woods," he said. "I can go with the girl."

"Thank you, sir," I whispered.

"You're welcome. I'm glad to be of service. But why do you need me so suddenly?"

We were already out the door and walking down the street.

"It's Mum," I said. "She's fainted at the factory."

"Fainted? Your mother? Goodness, child, I am beginning to get the feeling that your family is extremely weak of heart."

"Oh, never mind our hearts and their weaknesses! Mum needs you *now*."

"Alright, calm down. No need to get upset." His tone was so docile. I hardly could believe that he still did not understand the seriousness of the situation.

By now we had reached the factory. I had to almost push the doctor in through the door, who was still contemplating my family's weak hearts.

Mary met us in the hall.

"Go quickly," she said. "Your mother is not well."

She squeezed my hand, then led us into the factory room.

Mr. O' Neale sat beside Mum, who was still lying on the floor. He rose as we entered, and ushered the doctor over to her.

"She is very ill, Dr. Baylor," he said quietly.

"Well, I will do the best I can to make her better," he said in a seemingly cheerful voice. But he did not sound hopeful.

With Mr. O' Neale carrying Mum, we slowly made our way home. I dreaded seeing my sisters' faces as we approached the apartment building.

Robert was sitting on the step as we came up the street.

"Mum? Are you all right?" Turning to me, Robert asked, "Vi, what happened?"

"Mum just... fainted at the factory. We need to get her inside, quickly. Will you hold the door, Robert?"

He nodded silently.

110

Helen and Anna looked up in alarm when we entered the apartment, but Emma hushed their worried questions with assurances that Mum would be fine, they'd see.

Mum's pale form was laid gently on her bed. By now, it was getting to be evening time, and it was growing dark. I lit a candle so that the doctor could inspect Mum.

"Well, Violet, why don't you go now and make sure your sister has dinner ready? Your father will be quite famished when he comes home."

Mr. O' Neale's advice was wise, and so I left the room promptly, closing the door behind myself.

Sitting at the table, I waited impatiently for Dr. Baylor and Father to come out of Mum's room. Father had arrived, and we had explained to him, in as few words as was possible, the nightmare that was truth. With no words other than, "Eat, Violet," he had exited the room and gone to Mum's bedside. I heard the door slam behind him.

"Muddy boots that he didn't even pause to take off," Emma said softly to herself, scrubbing away the prints Father's boots had left on the floor. I saw a tear

111

drop from her eye and it dripped off of the end of her nose and onto the floor.

"Is Mummy going to die?"

Grace's innocent question was so unexpected that Helen dropped the kettle of soup. It hit the floor with a clang, splashing soup on the floor, the table, and on all of us. No one moved.

Emma walked slowly over to Grace and took the little girl's hands.

"We don't know, Gracie," she said. "But God does. And if it is His will, she will live."

"But why would He want Mummy to die?"

"I don't know, Grace. And I don't think He would *want* her to die. Sometimes things happen in this world that we can't understand. But He always has a plan. Never forget that, Gracie. And even if it is His will that Mummy dies,"—at this a tear ran out of Grace's eye—"we can know that God has a plan. And even when all else fails, He won't."

Anna had bent to wipe up the spilled soup, but Emma raised a hand to stop her.

"Leave it," she said.

112

"We need to pray for Mummy," Grace said in a decided voice.

"Yes, we do, Grace," Emma said softly.

We all gathered around Emma as she spoke of the fears that gripped all of our hearts.

When Emma had finished her prayer, the doctor entered. Gripping his hat and avoiding our eyes, he informed us that he could not cure our mother.

"But you said that you would make her better!" I cried.

"God is the only one who can truly heal your mother now."

I saw Emma's face, frozen in shock. She started weeping bitterly, the children surrounding her and clinging to her arms. I couldn't watch this. I left the room, and went into my bedroom.

I pulled out a piece of paper, intending to write to Lilli of this news. But as I put the pen to the paper all I could write, over and over, was

No, Mum, no, no, Mum, no!

CHAPTER 11

It rained one morning.

"Is the whole world crying for Mum?" Grace asked Emma.

Mum. She occupied our thoughts every minute of every hour. Her coughs filled the atmosphere of our small apartment. Dr. Baylor came and went, but he didn't speak a word to us. He only shook his head sadly when Emma asked if Mum was faring any better.

The details of Mum's illness were dreadful. Her body had been weakened severely by the continual heat and dust of the factory. With the coming cold weather, she had been susceptible to catching cold, and catch a cold was exactly what happened. Her fever raged, and she had no strength to fight it off. Dr. Baylor did not have much hope of her survival.

I sat at the table, slowly eating my breakfast without noticing what went in my mouth. Everyone wassilent, as though speaking a word would somehow be wrong in this great sorrow. Even Milky, lying by the warm kitchen stove, kept his purrs to a low sound.

Someone knocked on the door. Henry went to open it.

It was Ethan. He stood on the doorstep, an envelope in his hand and a merry smile on his face.

"I see you are fully recovered, Violet," he said.

"Yes, I am fine, thank you," I said dully.

"Violet, what is wrong?" He looked around the room at all of our melancholy faces.

Robert was the first to speak.

"It's Mum," he said. "She's *awful* sick."

"Sick?" Ethan asked, looking at me. Something strange burned in his eyes, something I couldn't quite understand. "How sick?"

"Almost dying," Anna said, tears spilling out of her eyes.

Violets Are Blue

"I'm sorry, Ethan, but it's really not the best time for you to come."

"Oh, yes, of course. My apologies. I only came to deliver this,"—he held up the envelope—"to you, Violet. I was down at the post office, and I saw that this had come in for you."

I took the envelope without glancing at it.

"It's from someone in Eastbourne..."

Immediately I turned my attention to the letter.

"... and I wasn't sure you knew anyone from Eastbourne. Do you?"

Helen spoke up quickly. "Lillian."

"Who's Lillian?"

"Lillian Prescott," I answered. Then I added, "She was my best friend."

"She *was* your best friend?"

"Well, she still is. It's just... she still lives in Eastbourne, and my family and I live here now. We write letters back and forth."

"Ah, so *that's* why I always see you going to the post office."

116

I blushed. I was always so eager for Lillian to get my replies that I rushed to the post office with my letter to her only a few hours after her letters arrived.

"Well, I'd better go now. I really hope your mother heals quickly, Violet," he said solemnly, and I could tell that he meant it. I wondered absentmindedly why Mum's health mattered so much to him.

He left quickly, closing the door behind himself.

I didn't bother to open Lilli's letter. At the moment, I could hardly stand to read her bubbly cheerfulness. But I kept it in a drawer by my bed, determined not to lose it. Someday, when Mum was well, I would read it.

Sorrow is inescapable. Even when I slept, my dreams reminded me of the truth. The scariest parts of these dreams were not as they should have been. There was nothing in them that the world would define as "frightening" or "scary." No nightmarish figures or others of that kind made me wake up shivering, as I always did.

117

Rather, it was the reality that scared me. The sorrow. The *words.* Dr. Baylor informing us of Mum's death; all of us at her mournful funeral, dressed in black; these images constantly flashed through my head in my restless slumber. The fact that all of these things could very well happen was the part that would scare me the most.

Mum made no progress, for better or worse. Her coughing stopped, giving place to much worse fevered exclamations. The doctor watched her constantly, but he spoke not a word. There was nothing he could do to help her.

We were not allowed to see Mum, for fear of catching the sickness. The doctor would not let us come into her room, especially not Grace, for she was very young. We all missed Mum dreadfully, but that could not be helped.

"The best way to help your mum is to let her rest so that she can regain her strength and heal," Dr. Baylor said over and over.

One morning, the doctor informed us that sometime this night, a change would come. Whether it

118

would be for the better or for the worse, he could not tell. But a change would come.

We all paced around the house that day, waiting. Emma was the only one who kept working, taking out her misery on the pots and pans and floor. Our house had never been cleaner, and it was all for the best, for the rest of us could do nothing that day. I sat in the rocking chair with Grace for hours, just rocking back and forth, my ears alert for any news from the doctor. The hours seemed to drag. Milky stalked the apartment, snapping at everyone.

At evening time, Emma tried to coax us to eat a bit of supper, but no one was hungry. Helen and Anna were pale-faced and anxious, their hands clenched together under the table; Robert and Henry had downcast faces as they attempted to eat a few bites of food; Grace was silently crying in her chair, her little shoulders shaking.

Just then Dr. Baylor entered and announced that he was going to go to his apartment for dinner.

"But I'll be back," he said. "I want to watch your mother and see how she progresses."

Emma thanked him quickly, and then he left.

Rain drizzled slowly down the windows. Ever since Mum became ill, it had rained constantly.

All this waiting was beginning to wear on me. I couldn't sit still, not knowing how Mum was doing, for another minute. I got up abruptly and left the table.

I ran down the apartment staircase quickly, eager to reach the door. Dashing outside, I stood in the rain and let it drench me thoroughly. The drops of water soaked me to the skin, soothing me a very small bit.

But I didn't stop for long. I was still running, although I didn't know to where I was going. The rain pounded on my back, soaking me even more. I shivered, remembering that it was early November and I was outside, wet and dripping, without a shawl or coat.

The rain was so hard that I could barely see the street in front of me. Raindrops washed everything out, making the buildings and automobiles on the street a blur. I shivered once more.

"Violet! What are ye doin' out here, lass?" I heard Mr. O' Neale's voice call out to me over the rain.

Turning, I realized suddenly where I was. The forge was right in front of me, giving off a pleasant heat.

"Violet!" Mr. O' Neale called again. "Come into the shop, lass, and warm up!"

I trudged, dripping, into his blacksmith forge. The fire that burned constantly warmed me up quickly and dried my hair. I held my hands out to the fire, feeling the heat tingle my fingers.

"What were ye doin' oot in that rain, lass?" Mr. O' Neale asked curiously.

"Oh," I said, not sure how to reply.

"Yer mam's not well yet, is she?" he asked.

I shook my head.

"I'm real sorry, Violet. But she'll get better. That mam of yers is strong. Just ye see—she'll live."

I shook my head again. "I'm not so sure, sir."

"It's no that bad, is it?"

I nodded.

He turned suddenly, and called, "Mary! Violet Bradshaw is here!"

Mary emerged from a back room in the forge.

"Hello, Violet," she said softly. "How's yer mam?"

"Well..." I said slowly. "She's not well."

"I'm sorry."

"Violet was out in the rain," he said. "Can ye git her a warm blanket?"

"Of course," Mary said. She ran out of the room and quickly returned with a thick gray blanket.

I took it gratefully, and wrapped myself up quickly.

"Why were ye oot in the rain, Violet?" Mary asked. Her green eyes were quizzical.

"Um, well..." I didn't know how to explain it.

"I think Violet was feeling a bit stressed after all the trouble with her mam," Mr. O' Neale explained.

"Oh, yes, I understand." Mary's voice was sympathetic.

"You do?"

"When me mam died a few winters ago, I didn't really feel like talking to anyone. All the kind ladies of the village swarmed 'round, a'tellin' me how sorry they were for me loss and such. At the time, I was so broken

122

hearted I was that their kind words seemed to scrape against me raw heart."

"Are you saying that you think Mum..."

"I'm not saying that I think yer mum will die. That's not what I meant by me words. I was tryin' to explain that I feel your pain. I understand what it feels like when a loved one is ill."

Oh. She understood. She had experienced the pain I was now experiencing.

And suddenly I was crying into her shoulder, harder then I ever had before. My tears came violently, and I sank to the floor. Mary rubbed my back and stroked my hair, attempting to sooth me, but I was not to be soothed.

"Oh, Mary," I wept. "What if she dies? I don't think I could bear it!"

"There, there."

"I... I can't let her go, Mary! I just can't!"

"I know that," she said.

I finally reached the point where I could cry no more.

"Thank you, Mary," I said, wiping my eyes.

"It's all right, Violet. I'm that glad to help I am."

I squeezed Mary's hand, thanked Mr. O' Neale
for letting me in from the rain, and left the warm
comforts of the forge.

CHAPTER 12

It was dark by the time I arrived home. Stars sparkled and winked in the sky. I glanced up at them. "So beautiful," I said in a whisper. My breath made a cloud in the chilly air.

A window squeaked open above me. Emma's head leaned out of it, her eyes relieved.

"Violet!" she said. "Oh, I'm so glad to see you! Where have you been? We were so worried."

"I... I was just out for a bit of fresh air," I explained.

"Oh, oh, of course," Emma said, although it seemed as though she had not heard a word I had said. "Come in quickly, Vi! You'll never believe..."

I didn't hear the rest, for I was already running up the stairs.

"What is it?" I asked Emma eagerly, upon reaching the apartment doorway.

"Mum," Emma said, two tears coming to her eyes.

I felt a sense of dread seep through me. Mum was dead. I hadn't had the chance to say goodbye. Mum was dead; she was *gone.* Just like in my nightmares.

But if Mum was dead, why was Emma smiling?

"Here," she said, taking my hand. "Come see her."

We entered Mum's room on tiptoe. She was in bed, her face pale and worn, but her blue eyes were radiant.

"Violet," she said softly, a smile coming to her face.

"Oh, Mum," I said, running into her arms.

She kissed my forehead gently. "I am so happy to see you again, Vi."

"Are you all better?"

"Not quite, dear. But I am healing. My fever has broken, and I will be all better soon."

Her words gave me more reassurance then I had felt in quite some time.

"I love you," I whispered in her ear.

"I love you, too, dear. I love you, too."

126

Elizabeth Rose

Mum is well!

These were the first words that came to mind as I sat to write a joyful letter to Lilli. Sometime in the midst of Mum's illness, I had taken the time to write my friend an epistle that explained all that was occurring. Her reply had been brief, but touching all the same:

Oh, Violet, I'm so sorry to hear about your mum. I'll be praying for you.

Your emotions right now remind me of a line from my mum's favorite hymn, "Nearer My God to Thee" —

"Though like the wanderer, the sun gone down,

Darkness be over me, my rest a stone;

Yet in my dreams I'd be nearer, my God, to Thee,

Nearer, my God, to Thee, nearer to Thee!"

Seek Him, Violet—cling to Him. Always, when you feel this terrible fear that your mum may die, draw nearer to God. You must not lose sight of the One who holds life and death in His hands. Through our saddest times, through the worst of tragedies, He alone can be the balm for our aching hearts.

Love,

Lilli

Now I resolved to write a joyful reply to her, informing her of the happy news.

Oh Lilli, Mum is healed! She is well, and on the mend. Oh Lilli, I'm so happy. It's too wonderful.

I could think of nothing more to say, so great was my happiness.

128

Mum healed slowly but steadily. Dr. Baylor checked in on her daily, and he came out of her room with a broad smile on his face each time.

"She's doing well," he would say. "Only a few more days."

"Only a few more days?" I commented to Emma impatiently several days later. "When will Mum be well?"

"Oh, Violet," she said, pulling a loaf of bread from the oven. "Be patient. Mum is healing, and that's what matters." She lightly placed her finger on top of the loaf. "Take this and put it on that shelf to cool, will you? I don't want Grace or Henry burning themselves."

I took the bread from her, using a towel to shield my hands from the heat, and placed it on the shelf. Then I sat down at the table once more.

"Emma?"

"Yes?"

"Have you seen a letter sitting around the house addressed to me?"

"Why?"

"I've lost Lillian's letter, the one Ethan delivered when Mum was so sick." I sighed. "Or at least I think I have. I can't think where I could have put it!"

"Why, haven't you read it yet, Vi?"

"No, I have not. I felt sure that I couldn't stand to read it just then, with Mum being so ill and all."

"Then why did you send her the letter about Mum's sickness?"

"Because I felt she had a right to know. And I read her reply to *that* letter. It's just this one—the letter Ethan brought. I just wasn't in the mood to read it at the time, and so I put it away to read later."

"Have you looked everywhere?"

"Yes, everywhere! I've searched the apartment high and low. It's not to be found."

"Oh dear. I'll keep an eye out for it."

"Thank you." I paced around the room, restless.

"Emma?"

"Hmm?" Her mouth was full of pins, for she had sat down to do the mending.

"How can you bear waiting?"

"You could help out with the chores a bit more," she said, a teasing smile on her face. "Keeping occupied helps time go by."

"I guess you're right." I sighed. "What do you need help with?"

"You could stop by the butcher's."

"Of course," I said. At least it was something to *do.*

"Oh, and Violet?" she added, turning.

"Yes?" I said impatiently, already halfway out the door.

"Please don't buy the whole store."

"I won't," I said, pretending to scowl.

The fresh air outside did do me worlds of good, and the walk to the butcher's invigorated me. I entered the shop and took a deep breath, my eyes trailing over the walls and shelves.

"Yes?"

It was Mr. Peterson, the butcher. He stood behind the counter, an expectant look on his face.

"Oh, yes, um, I came to get meat, sir," I said quickly, blushing in my embarrassment.

131

"That's what the majority do when they come to the butcher's." He was pretending to be stern, but his eyes sparkled.

"Of—of course, sir. May I have a minute, please? I'm not sure what I'm going to purchase quite yet."

"Certainly." He turned and motioned to someone in the backroom. "Help the girl, Ethan. I've got some lamb to chop into quarters."

"Of course, Uncle George," Ethan said, smiling broadly. "How are you today, Violet?"

"Fine, actually."

"You say that every day."

"Really?" I hadn't realized that.

"Is your mother..."

"Mum is doing much better. The worst of the sickness is over, and she's on the mend. I know I should be glad that she's healing, but... well, it's hard to wait."

"You're so impatient, Violet." He grinned again. "What did your letter say?"

"My letter?"

"I believe it was from a young lady named Lillian Prescott...?"

132

"Yes. My letter. Um, well..."

"Haven't you read it yet?"

"No, no, I haven't. I put it away—somewhere—when Mum was still sick. Now I have no idea where it could be."

"You lost it?"

"No, I didn't lose it! I just *misplaced* it."

"Well, just let me know when you *re*place it."

I rolled my eyes, and sighed in exasperation. "Do you have any fresh lamb?" I said briskly, trying to change the subject.

"Uh, yes, we do, but it's pretty expensive. I'm not sure if..."

"How much is the lamb, Ethan?"

"Well, it just so happens that today this lamb is on sale, exclusively, for a certain Miss Bradshaw."

"Oh, really? And what will your uncle say to that?"

"He'll say 'Good work, Ethan. That's how you get customers to come back!' "

I rolled my eyes, paid for the meat, took the brown parcel he handed me and left the shop.

"Did you get the meat?" Emma asked as I arrived home.

"Yes. I got lamb."

"Lamb?" She looked alarmed. "Violet, I told you not to buy the whole store! Lamb is expensive..."

"Ethan gave it to me for cheap."

"Oh. That was generous of him."

"Yes, it was."

I handed her the parcel, then marched out of the room, intent on finding my letter. Emma called as I was leaving the kitchen:

"Oh, and Violet, I had a thought while you were at the butchers about the location of your letter. I remembered you putting it in your drawer by your bed, when Mum was still sick. Do you think it's still there?"

My bed! The drawer! That's where I had put the letter from Lilli!

"Thank you, Emma!" I called, rushing to the bedroom and starting to rapidly search through my drawer.

"You're welcome," she answered. Even though I couldn't see her face, I could tell from her voice that she was smiling.

Suddenly, my fingers brushed an envelope. I felt the hard seal on the back, then flipped it over in the light where I could see it. The letter was addressed to a Miss Violet Bradshaw. I opened it quickly, the envelope falling to the floor unnoticed. The letter was written in Lilli's unmistakable handwriting:

Dear Violet,

Oh, you will never guess. I just know that you will never be able to guess this news that I have for you. I will tell you now, and save you the curiosity. As you know, we are to come to America as soon as Father earns enough money to pay our fare. But you'll never guess on what ship we shall cross the ocean! It is the Titanic herself! Imagine that? The greatest, biggest, most luxuriant ship in the world, and I am going to cross the ocean on it! Just think of the adventure! Of course, we shall have to travel in third class, but it will still be grand.

Isn't this just positively wonderful?

Love,

Lillian

Lillian was right. This *was* positively wonderful, more wonderful than I ever could have imagined.

CHAPTER 13

I awoke early the next morning. The birds had ceased their chirping by now and had all flown south, for it was nearly December, which meant Christmas. I wondered if we'd be able to afford any kind of a feast this year. Last year we had been saving our money for the voyage across the sea, so we had had no money for extras. I hoped this year would be different, but with Mum's doctor bills, I couldn't be very hopeful.

Glancing at the clock, I realized that it was time for me to be getting to the factory. Mum would not be coming back to the factory for some time, but I was fully fit, and had been for several days, and I intended to get back to work.

I rose out of bed quickly, searching in the gray light for my clothes. It was chilly with no fire burning in the kitchen stove, and I stood there, shivering, for a minute. Then my hands brushed the fabric of my skirt, and I dressed quickly, still shivering. I braided my hair swiftly, then tiptoed out of the room.

The apartment stairs creaked as I trudged down them, and I wished I knew how to go down them without hitting all the squeaky spots. Robert could do this, and he had promised to show me one time. I had noticed that Mum was also quite capable in this skill.

It was even colder outside, and I rubbed my hands together, wishing I had remembered a pair of mittens. The factory was not far and for once, its heat was not a burden, although I knew very well that it would quickly start to weigh on me over the course of the day.

I opened the door to the factory and walked into the room where I worked. Mary was there, and she waved one hand at me cheerfully, while using the other to guide her fabric through the machine. I waved back, then sat in my usual seat by my machine.

The hours went by slowly. At noon I looked at the clock, worked for about ten minutes more, then glanced at the clock again. It was time for Mr. Woods to come and do his usual rounds, for it was Friday. Finally I turned to Mary.

"It's Friday—shouldn't Mr. Woods be here soon?"

"Are ye that hopeful to git slapped again?" Mary grinned.

"No, but it's his normal time to come and check that we are doing our work right."

"Didn't you hear?" A girl across the room had been listening in on the conversation.

"Didn't I hear what?" I asked.

"Mr. Woods. He's not coming back. His wife's just given birth."

"What?"

"Didn't you hear?" She looked at me as if anyone in their right mind would have heard about this news already.

"Stop saying that!" I jumped out of my seat in my frustration. "I *didn't* hear—you know that! Now what happened with Mrs. Woods?"

"She gave birth to a little baby girl just a few nights ago."

"Oh." I sank back down into my seat.

"Do ye know what they named the bairn?" Mary asked the stranger girl.

"No—do you?"

"No. Violet, do you know?"

"No, I don't," I answered. "I'm just hearing all of this now."

"Ah, yes, o' course, Vi," Mary said kindly. "Now we'd best get back to work."

I was eager to tell Mum the news as soon as I arrived home.

"Mrs. Woods had a baby!"

"Oh, that's wonderful! But when did she give birth?"

"I'm not sure."

"Who told you this news?"

"Mary, and another girl at the factory."

"How did they know?"

"I—I don't know."

"Do you know what she named the baby?"

"No—they didn't know either."

"We should send them over a basket of food, and perhaps a blanket for the baby."

"But Mum, Mr. Woods was so..."

"Forgiveness is a virtue, Vi." She smiled at me. "Now, go inform Emma of the good news!"

I dashed into the kitchen, where Emma was feeding Milky. "Emma, Mrs. Woods..."

"... Had a baby, I know!" She grinned. "I could hear you from Mum's room! Are you always so loud when you're excited?"

"Mum suggested that we make up a basket for the baby," I said, then added, "and for the parents as well, of course."

"You're still not so fond of Mr. Woods, are you?"

"No, and I do not expect to ever like him that much. But Mum says we should forgive him."

"And Mum is right, of course. Here." She handed me a basket. "As I said, I could hear you from

Mum's room. And so, I made this up for you to take to the Woods."

I peaked inside. Emma had placed a loaf of fresh bread, a few jars of raspberry preserves, some butter biscuits, a blanket, and a baby's bonnet all in the basket.

"How did you?—when did you make the bonnet and blanket?"

"I've had a little extra time." She winked at me. "Besides, when you told me that Mrs. Woods had been out of the factory for some time... and you did tell me that she was quite stout when you first met her... well, I assumed that she was with child."

I left the apartment with the heavy basket, and walked down the street to the Woods' apartment. I noticed once more that it was in a far nicer location then our apartment, and I hoped that the meager gifts of the less fortunate would not be looked down upon. Taking a deep breath, I walked bravely up the stairs.

I heard strains of hearty laughter coming from behind the Woods' door. *That's odd,* I thought. *Mr. Woods is laughing?*

He was indeed. As I knocked briskly on the door, I could hear his guffawing even clearer.

The maid led me down the hall, to the room that Mrs. Woods had occupied the last time I had seen her.

"She's in there, miss. Please don't disturb her— she's resting."

I promised that I would do my best not to fatigue Mrs. Woods, and then I entered the room.

"Mrs. Woods?"

"Violet," she smiled up from the pillows. Her face was tired, but happy. "Come and see my little girl."

"I brought a basket of... things you may need for the baby."

"Thank you, dear child," she said, while squeezing my hand. "You can put it over there."

"May I hold her?" I asked, after placing the basket on a small table.

"Of course."

She placed the baby in the crook of my arm. I looked down in wonder at the tiny infant. Her features were absolutely perfect. "What did you name her?"

"We named her Abigail," she answered, smiling up at her husband.

"Abby," I whispered. "What a pretty name."

I heard footsteps and turned to see Mr. Woods standing behind me, a somewhat sheepish look on his face.

"I'd like to apologize, Miss Bradshaw," he said. "I know you must think I'm a monster, for how I've treated your mother. It's just... well, the missus here was gettin' mighty close to the end of her pregnancy. I was worried for her, Miss Bradshaw," he admitted. "I was very frightened that I was gonna lose my dear wife. And I've been known for losin' my temper before, miss. You know that. It all just started to weigh down on me at that moment. It wasn't yer mother. She's a good worker; both of you are. I'm real sorry, miss.

"I won't be comin' back to the factory, miss," he continued. "You'll have a new boss, and I'll see that he treats you and your friends well, mark my words. I'm really, really sorry. Will you forgive me?"

I still couldn't speak. Mr. Woods was apologizing—to *me*.

"Oh, sir," I said. "I don't think I deserve your praise. I was awfully impudent to you at times."

"No, no," Mr. Woods said. "The fault is mine."

"Alright, alright, you two," Mrs. Woods interrupted. "Miss Violet didn't come over here to listen to you rave on and on about how sorry you are. Although,"—and at this she winked at me—"Violet is quite right when she said she was a bit impudent. She would be the first one I've ever see stand up to you, Frank!" She smiled. "I always thought you were spirited, Miss Violet Bradshaw. Remember the day I said you reminded me of our Nellie?"

I nodded, remembering as well.

She motioned for me to lean closer to her, then whispered in my ear: "Nellie's mighty spirited, she is... that is, for a horse!"

Mr. Woods' voice boomed with laughter, and Mrs. Woods and I joined him.

Violets Are Blue

I wrote a letter to Lilli as soon as I got home, telling about Mr. Woods apology.

I was so shocked. I couldn't believe it. I never, in my wildest dreams, thought Mr. Woods would apologize to me. At times I felt as though he almost killed Mum with his brutality. I thought I could never forgive him. And yet... when he asked for forgiveness, I forgave him. I don't know how it happened. The words seemed to come as if they were spoken by someone else.

I can't explain it, Lilli. In that one moment, when Mr. Woods asked for my forgiveness, something changed in my heart. It's something one can't put into words. All I know is that all my bitterness towards Mr. Woods melted. Just like that.

CHAPTER 14

The days wore by slowly, and pretty soon, Mum could be moving around just like before her illness. It made me so happy to see her well once more.

"I'm just going down to the post office, to mail a letter to Lillian," I informed Mum one evening, after having arrived home from the factory.

"The post's closed, dear," Mum said. "I know you want to help by taking on extra hours at the factory to help us scrape by, but... you don't need to work *so* much."

"Mum, now you sound like me before your illness!"

"And now I know how you felt. You were right, Violet. That factory could have killed me, and I wouldn't have even noticed it."

Even things at the factory were starting to look a bit brighter. The new owner and boss, Mr. Taylor, was fair and just. He was strict, but he never slapped me or Mary nor anyone else. The heat still plagued me, but I knew that this trouble would only last for a time. Soon, very soon, we would be quitting at the factory, for Mr. Prescott had earned enough money to get his family across the sea, as was revealed in Lilli's letter to me. Mum would never have to work at that factory again, even with its improvements. God was so good to us.

Everything seemed to be going so smoothly and pleasantly. The only problem was Christmas. I knew in my heart that our first Christmas here in America should be special. But I was also painfully aware of our lack of funds for extra treats... and a ham for Christmas was certainly more than just an extra treat.

I decided to talk to Emma about it; she always had good ideas. It was she who suggested saving up money for Mum's new apron, after all. But that project had been forgone for quite some time, ever since the factory entered our lives.

"Emma?" I called, entering the bedroom.

She was not there. I turned to Helen and Anna, who were sitting on the floor with their dolls.

"Helen, Anna, have either of you seen Emma?"

149

Violets Are Blue

Anna turned to Helen with a quizzical look on her face.

"Now that you mention it..." she said. "I haven't seen Emma all morning. Helen, have you?"

Helen shook her head, her long brunette braids shaking.

"No, I haven't. But why do you need Emma, Vi?"

"I wanted to ask her a question about Christmas."

"Christmas! Oh, I almost forgot! Is it really so close?" Helen's eyes shone with excitement.

"Christmas is in only in one more week," Anna counted on her fingers. "We don't have much time to make a feast."

"A feast! Will there really be a feast?" Helen and Anna both turned to me eagerly.

"Well, girls, that's what I wanted to talk about with Emma." I sat down on the floor next to them. "You see, we don't have very much money for a feast... and..."

"No feast? But it's Christmas—we have to have a feast!" Helen's face looked sadly disappointed.

150

"It's all right, Violet. We understand," Anna said softly. "Don't we, Helen?"

"Understand? But that's not fair! It's not Christmas without a ham! Can we not afford just a small one?" Helen looked very upset.

"I don't know," I sighed. "But I don't think we should worry Mum and Father about it. If they see that we're disappointed, it will make them feel really bad that they can't afford a ham."

"Yes," Anna said. "I won't say anything. I don't want to hurt Mum or Father."

Helen just frowned.

"Well, I'd best go see if I can find Emma," I said, rising to my feet. "Don't worry, Helen," I reassured my sister. "We'll make this Christmas special no matter what."

Emma was nowhere to be found. I searched high and low, and I even asked Mum, but she had not seen her.

"Maybe she's down by the harbor!" Robert suggested eagerly.

"I highly doubt that," I said, imagining my sweet and proper older sister down by the damp and fishy-smelling harbor.

Just then the door opened. Emma stood in the doorway, grinning.

"Emma!" I said in relief. "I've looked everywhere! Where have you been?"

"Calm down, Violet. I'm here now, see? And as to where I've been... well, you shall have to wait a while to learn that, for I cannot reveal all of my secrets."

"Oh, never mind where you've been. I need to talk to you about something."

I grabbed my sister's hand and practically dragged her to our room, where we could talk in private. Helen and Anna had left the room ten minutes earlier, and it was now empty.

"Violet, what is it?" Emma asked in frustration. "You needn't drag me from the room like that. I would have come."

"Yes, you would have come... but not quickly enough."

"How many times have I told you to be more patient?" Emma scolded.

"I didn't drag you in here to talk about my patience..."

"...Or rather, your lack thereof," Emma replied with a smirk.

"That's not the point," I said, blushing. "Emma, please listen."

"I'm listening." She sat down on our bed, and I sat beside her.

"Well, with Christmas coming ..." I began.

Just then Henry popped his head in through the doorway.

"Hi, Emma!" he said. "Vi was lookin' for you."

"And I found her," I answered. "Now Henry, please leave—I need to discuss something with Emma."

"Well, if you're going to share secrets, I'm not leaving." Henry crossed his arms over his chest, a determined look on his face.

I sighed. "Perhaps this would be easier if we went somewhere else."

"If you leave, I'm comin' too," Henry said.

"Henry, if you let us talk now, I will tell you a story when we get back," Emma promised.

"Really?"

"Yes. But please, let us talk."

"Alright..." And Henry left the room.

"Let's go out on the fire escape," I suggested.

"Good idea."

The wind was frigid outside, and we both were shivering, but at least we had privacy now.

"Now Violet, what were you saying about Christmas?"

"That's exactly it. Christmas." I sighed drearily as I glanced over the streets that were several stories below us. "I know we have no money for an expensive feast, Emma," I said. "But it's our first Christmas here in America, and it would be so special if, somehow, we could." I sighed once more. "I know the children, especially Helen, will be very disappointed if we don't have a ham."

154

"I understand," Emma said slowly. "But we don't have the money. That's the simple truth."

"I know," I said. "But I thought we could, well... earn the money."

"Violet, do you have any idea how much a ham, especially at this time of year, costs?"

"Yes, I do. And I know it will take a while, but we have time..."

"We have a week," Emma interrupted.

"Then it's hopeless, isn't it?"

Emma smiled. "I wouldn't say *hopeless*..."

She entered the apartment, then reappeared with a covered basket.

"Open it," she said softly, glancing around to make sure no one was looking.

I lifted the linen that was covering the basket, then gasped.

Arranged neatly inside the basket were several scarves, sets of mittens, and even hats!

"How... how..."

"Remember when I said that I've had some extra time? Besides little Abby's things, I've been making

155

these as well. I figured that we might be able to sell them in order to earn enough money to buy a ham, and maybe a few other things—like presents—for Christmas."

"Oh, Emma, that's a splendid idea!" I said, flinging my arms around her in a hug.

"I thought so. But I need your help," she whispered. "I need you to keep knitting scarves, mittens, hats—anything that you can think of that might be needed in the winter. I will do the selling."

"Is that where you were when you said 'and as to where I've been, you shall have to wait awhile to learn that, for I cannot reveal all my secrets'?"

Emma nodded, smiling. "I was selling a few of my wares."

We were interrupted by Mum's voice:

"Girls, supper is ready!"

As we entered the kitchen, we smiled at each other in a secretive manner.

"What have you two been up to out on the fire escape for all that time?" Mum asked, her eyes merry.

"Discussing matters of little importance," Emma replied lightly, smiling back at Mum. "Christmas *is* coming, after all."

"You promised to tell me a story!" Henry reminded Emma.

She rumpled his hair. "And I intend to keep that promise. I will tell you a story as soon as we finish supper."

"Alright..." Henry conceded.

"What's for supper, Mum?" Helen asked as she and Anna entered the room. Their cheeks were red and rosy, and their matching brown braids were rumpled.

"Where have you two been?" Emma asked.

"Secrets," Anna answered in a mysterious tone.

"Indeed," I replied, winking at Emma.

Just then, Robert entered the room.

"Is supper ready, Mum? I'm starving!"

"Yes, supper is ready, son. We're just going to wait for your father. He should be home soon."

Father arrived home about five minutes later, and we all sat down at the table to eat the delicious vegetable soup and fresh bread. Glancing around the table at all the happy faces of my family, I realized that it was not exactly a necessity that we have a ham for Christmas. We would have a wonderful Christmas no matter what—just because we were here, safe and warm, together.

But I still wanted to get a ham, if it was possible.

CHAPTER 15

Christmas made New York beautiful. Garlands hung in shop windows, the toy store was filled with shiny-new dolls, soldiers, and other playthings, and the candy shops proudly displayed ornate gingerbread houses in their windows. The snow just added to the magical feeling about everything, and with the soft strains of Christmas music coming from the shops, I realized that there actually *were* things to like about this city.

"Thank you! Thank you very much!" Emma smiled cheerily at our most recent customer.

The old lady on her apartment's doorstep smiled, nodded, then closed the door, holding in her hands the knitted scarf she had just bought from us.

"How many have we sold?" I asked Emma curiously as we walked down the street in the freezing cold. Our cheeks were rosy red; our eyes bright as we walked quickly to stay warm. The wind was brisk and chilly, and I rubbed my hands together to keep them warm, for my mittens were worn and thin.

"That's ten, I think," Emma said uncertainly, counting on her fingers. "And then I sold three pair of mittens the first day..."

"But how much money is that?" I asked eagerly.

"Well, the scarves are two cents, and the mittens are a penny. We've sold three pairs of mittens and six scarves, so that's a grand total of..."

"Fifteen cents!" I interrupted. "How much is the ham?"

"I believe ham is nineteen cents," Emma said slowly. "I'm not sure, though—I haven't been to the butcher's in quite some time."

"Well, we're passing the butcher's now, so you can check," I said. "Oh, I do hope it is less than fifteen cents!"

We had reached the cheery butcher shop, which was decked out in all of its holiday finery. Garlands and berries hung from the shelves, and a huge wreath was on the door. Ethan was shoveling the snow away from the street in front of the shop as we approached, and he

160

smiled at us, all the while pushing his shovel over the sidewalk.

"Hello, ladies," he said politely.

"Hello, Mr. Hartley," Emma replied, her courteous tone matching his. She still insisted on calling him by the name that proper manners dictated. "We've come to purchase a ham. How much would they be?"

"The hams?" Ethan looked uncertain, then opened the door to the butcher shop. "Uncle George, how much are the hams?" he asked Mr. Peterson, who was standing at the counter.

"The hams are nineteen cents," Mr. Peterson answered, without looking up from the ledger in which he was writing.

"There you have it," Ethan said. "Nineteen cents."

"Oh," I sighed in disappointment. "We have only fifteen cents."

"I could..." Ethan started to say.

"No, don't trouble yourself, Mr. Hartley," Emma interrupted. "I am sure we can come back another time."

"Alright, then," Ethan said, going into the shop.

"Emma, we have but fifteen!" I exclaimed, as we continued on our way. "If Ethan is willing to..."

"Violet, that wouldn't be right. We cannot take advantage of them. If they do not get paid full price for their meat, they will have no way of living." Emma turned to me, a smile on her face that seemed somewhat forced. "It is all as it should be, Vi," she said calmly.

My shoulders drooped. As Emma had pointed out, we had sold only nine items. We had soon found out that not many people had been willing to pay good money for scarves and mittens that they could have easily made themselves. And now, only two days before Christmas Eve, we were four cents short. I had so wanted to surprise Mum and Father with a ham, but it could not be helped—we would have no ham for Christmas this year. Emma and I trudged home slowly, sadly disappointed.

"Girls!" Mum called out of the window as we approached the apartment building. "Girls, come inside quickly!"

"What is it, Mum?" Emma asked.

"Just come inside, girls," Mum insisted. She said nothing more, and closed the window with a *thump.*

I looked at Emma curiously, then we both ran up the apartment stairs.

"Here, put it here," Mum was saying, her voice coming from behind what seemed to be a small, scrawny tree. Father was moving the tree into the main room of the apartment, and Mum was moving the chairs out of his way.

"A tree!" Helen exclaimed, clapping her hands in delight. "A real Christmas tree!"

"But, how..." I stammered in bewilderment, staring in shock at the tree that was now standing in the middle of the room.

"Father got a tree!" Anna added excitedly.

"Yes, but how?" Emma asked, coming up behind me with her scarf and coat in her arms.

"I don't know either," Mum commented, looking to Father, a question in her eyes.

"Now, now, it's Christmas," Father said, a broad smile on his face. "Am I expected to give away all of my secrets?"

Helen groaned. "*Please?*" she begged.

"It's a secret," Father repeated, winking at her.

"I'm still extremely curious how Father ever got such a tree," Emma said, brushing the now-melting snow from her long brunette curls.

"Your father has always loved surprises," Mum said. "I wouldn't be surprised if he's been planning this since July, actually. *Where* he would get a tree is what puzzles me."

"It puzzles me as well," I confided. "But, it is a hopeless case, is it not?"

"I fear that it is," Mum said, smiling at the both of us. "Your father, as I've said, has always loved surprises. And, because he loves surprises so much, he has an exceptional talent for keeping secrets."

"Why is Father so secretive about the tree?" Helen asked as she entered the warm kitchen where we sat, drinking hot tea.

"I don't know, dearest," Mum said, brushing Helen's hair with her hand. Helen flinched away from her touch.

"But can he not tell us where he got it?" Helen whined.

"Helen," Mum said, turning to my little sister. "Does anyone require that you tell where you get the presents you give out at Christmas?"

"No, that wouldn't be fair!" Helen said. "If they knew, it wouldn't be so surprising."

"Think of Father's tree as a Christmas gift to all of us. By insisting that he tell you where he got the tree, you are demanding that he tell you his secrets. You of all people, Helen, should know that that would not be fair."

"No..." Helen admitted, a frown on her face. "But I'm *curious*, Mum!"

"I am, too," Mum said. "But our curiosity does not give us a good excuse to demand that Father inform us where or when he got the lovely tree." She smiled at Helen, who gave a weak smile back. "Here, perhaps we should decorate it now."

"Decorate it?" Helen asked, her eyes lighting up.

"Indeed," Mum said, rising from her chair. "Call your brothers and sisters, Helen. I'll make some popcorn that we can string on thread to make a chain."

Helen dashed from the room, calling for Anna eagerly.

"Helen, my Helen," Mum sighed, a smile on her face. "You know I was just like that at her age, don't you?"

"Really?" Emma said, turning to Mum curiously.

"Ah, yes," Mum said, still smiling. "Always concerned with what was "fair." After a time, I had to learn that everything in this world was not going to be fair." She sighed once more. "Helen will learn the lesson one day as well."

That afternoon was very jolly; we all were gathered in the kitchen, making decorations for the tree. Mum made popcorn, and Helen and Anna strung it on a string. Henry and Robert eagerly ran outside into the cold with me, to gather stray pinecones for decorating. Angels were cut from fabric scraps and hung on the tree, the pinecones were decked out with red ribbons, and the popcorn string was finally complete. Mum stood to light

166

the candles carefully, and we all drew in our breath in amazement. The tree was a thing of beauty, warmly lighting the corner of the main room that served as our kitchen and sitting room.

"Finished!" Mum said, smiling around the room at all of our bright faces. "Your father will be very pleased."

"Where are the hams?" I asked in amazement, staring in the butcher's window. The hams that had hung in the front window for weeks were suddenly gone.

Mr. Peterson came to the door.

"All sold," he said.

"Even the last one?"

"Ah... yes, it was sold as well," Mr. Peterson said, turning a bit red in the face. I wondered what ailed him.

"Oh," I said in disappointment. Even though I knew we couldn't afford a ham, I still had hoped that, by some sort of miracle, we would have been able to get one.

"I'm sorry, miss, they're sold," Mr. Peterson insisted. "Was there anything else you needed?"

"No," I said softly.

I left the shop quietly and trudged down the street, my shoulders slumped and my spirit dejected.

Climbing the stairs to our apartment on the third floor, I noticed a rather large brown package sitting by our apartment door. I ran the rest of the way up the stairs and as I grew closer, realized that the package was a ham!

It was wrapped in a bright red ribbon, with a card, on which the words "*Merry Christmas*" were printed. Nothing else was on the ham, no indication at all of whom had given such a gift. I gaped at it in surprise, then started banging on the door.

"Mum! Emma! Come!" I called.

The door opened quickly. "Vi, whatever is the matter?" Emma asked in surprise. "The neighbors will be bothered—" Then she saw the ham. "Oh—oh, how did you..."

"A ham!" Helen exclaimed, peaking around the door. "A ham for Christmas! Oh, how wonderful!"

168

"What's all the commotion about?" Mum questioned, coming to the door. Then she too saw the ham, and was thus rendered speechless.

"It's a ham, Mum, a real ham for Christmas!" Helen exclaimed once more. "Isn't it wonderful?!"

"Yes, but how..." Mum asked, finding her voice. "Vi, did you..."

"It wasn't I, Mum! I am just as confused as you. I just found it—here on our doorstep—now. It doesn't have a name on it—no sign of who could have given it to us."

"But who would give such a gift?"

None of us knew the answer to that question.

"Well, here Emma, help me lift it to the kitchen table," Mum said. "Goodness, it's large, isn't it?"

When Father arrived home that night, he was not as amazed as we had expected.

"I was beginning to get a bit suspicious when all the hams in the butcher shop mysteriously disappeared," he confessed.

"But was it you, Father?" I asked.

"No, it wasn't I," he said. "But, whoever it was obviously wanted to keep his identity a secret. So,"—and

169

this with a wink towards Helen—"I think we should simply thank the Lord for this wondrous gift, and not concern ourselves with its whereabouts."

CHAPTER 16

"Violet, Violet, wake up, wake up!" Helen's voice was urgent, and it erased all sleep from my head. I sat up quickly with a jolt, my eyes wide with fear.

"What is it, Helen?" I asked urgently. "Is someone ill? Is something wrong?"

"Nothing's wrong, you silly," Emma said, smiling at me. She had come over to my bed and sat down on the edge. Her long brunette curls were still tangled from sleep, and reaching to her waist, rather than being twisted in her usual bun. "Helen was just teasing, dear."

"No I wasn't!" Helen said forcefully. "It's Christmas! The most wonderful day of the entire year!"

"The most wonderful day of the *year*?" Emma echoed. "I'm not sure, Helen—I mean, the first day of summer is lovely as well..."

"Not as lovely as Christmas!" Helen insisted. "Or at least, not as lovely to *me*."

Emma grinned. "You never change, Helen."

"I wish she'd change," Anna complained in a grouchy voice. "Helen woke me up at *five o' clock* this morning. Five o' clock! I'm telling Mum."

"Oh, it wasn't *five*," Helen said sheepishly. "It was, um... ten after five."

"And that really makes such a difference!" Anna said sarcastically. Her blue eyes seemed to snap angrily.

"Anna..." Emma spoke softly, a warning tone in her voice.

"Don't tell me what to do, Emma! If Helen hadn't awoken me at five o' clock, I'd have been able to..."

"You would have been able to do what?"

Anna jumped, startled. Father was standing in the doorway, grinning.

"I... I... I would have been able to get more sleep, um, last night, uh..." Anna floundered for words. Her face was bright red with embarrassment, for she had not intended for Father to overhear her words.

172

"Hmm..." Father mused. "Is what your sister says true, Helen?"

Helen gulped, then nodded. "Yes, sir."

Father turned to Helen with a small smile. "Then I have something to tell you."

"What?" Helen's chocolate-brown eyes were huge.

"I was just like you when I was young. I would be so eager to wake on Christmas morning, and I wanted to push that eagerness on all of my siblings as well. I was a great trial to them." Father shook his head, a small smile on his face. "My sister, Alice, also grew weary of my teasing. And so, one morning, when I was sound asleep, she awoke me... at four o' clock in the morning."

"Aunt Alice did that?" Henry had now entered the room, and he was listening to the story wide-eyed.

"Yes, she did. And you don't know how upset I was. Furiously, I flew at her, angry and wondering why she would wake me up at such an unnatural hour." At this he paused, turning his face towards his engrossed children. "Do you know what your aunt looks like?"

"Of course," Anna said. "She has curly blonde hair, and she's only about five feet tall."

"Yes," said Father. "Your aunt has always been very tiny. But yet, she was always full of such spirit. When I flew at her in anger, she stood her ground and spoke but a few words. And yet those few words pierced my heart."

"What did she say?"

"Alice is very wise. She simply faced me boldly, and in a whisper said, 'Am I any different than you?'"

"She said that? But what did she mean, Father?" Robert asked.

"She meant '*Why do you get angry at* me—*you have awoken all of us a thousand times and we never flew at you this way.*'"

Helen's face looked frozen in remorse. She ran over to where Anna was standing and gave her a fierce hug. "I'm so sorry, Anna," she said. "Can you *ever* forgive me?" She laid a hand dramatically to her brow.

Anna smiled and rolled her eyes at the gesture. "That's all right, Helen. I forgive you."

"What happened?" Mum asked. Her eyes looked tired, as though she had just woken up.

"Oh, nothing," Anna said, a mischievous look in her eye as she glanced at Helen. "Helen just woke me up at four o' clock!"

"What?" Now Mum looked very confused.

"Don't worry, Mum," I said. "Let's go eat breakfast."

Our tree had a small pile of presents underneath it, at which we gazed with wonder and excitement in our eyes. Mum, now dressed, handed out several packages.

"There is one present for each," she said. "I am sorry dears, but that is all we could afford."

"Don't worry about it, Mum," Emma spoke up quickly. "Thank you."

Grace was already eagerly tearing through the paper of her package. "Girls!" she shouted joyfully.

"*Paper dolls,*" Anna corrected. "Look Gracie, there's one with curls just like you!"

"Ooh!" Grace's face wore a huge grin.

"A ship!" Robby's eyes gleamed as he unwrapped the somewhat small model. "I'll put it by my bed! Father, could we take it down to the wharf today?"

Father nodded.

"I can't wait to see if it floats! Oh Father, a real ship! Just like the *Titanic*! I wonder how many people she could hold? I'm going to call her..."

"Oh, do be quiet, Robby," Helen snapped. She was glumly staring down at something red in her hands. "You don't need to prattle on so. You're being *rude*."

Robert shut his mouth with an audible *click*. Mum glanced towards Father, who slowly shook his head.

"Helen, what have you received?" Father asked, his voice sounding cheery.

"This," she answered, motioning unenthusiastically towards the pair of red mittens in her lap. "Just mittens. Plain, uninteresting mittens."

Anna nudged Helen with her elbow.

"I got blue mittens!" Anna said in a cheerful voice. "Just what I needed—my other pair was worn thin. And in my favorite color, too! Thank you, Mum."

Mum beamed at Anna, then turned to Grace, who was struggling with her paper dolls.

"I got a green scarf!" Henry said, with a big grin on his face. He proudly displayed it in his left hand.

I saw Anna out of the corner of my eye nudge Helen, who quickly nodded and then stood up.

"We have a gift for everyone," she said grandly. "Bring them in, Helen!"

Anna dashed out of the room, and then reappeared with a large crate. Inside, resting on a quilt, were many small pillows.

"What are they?" I asked curiously.

"Oh, you silly—don't you know?" Anna asked. "It's a sachet!" She held up one of the little pillows, and then handed it to Mum. "Here Mum—sniff it."

Mum sniffed carefully, and then a smile came to her face. "Oh, what a sweet gift, girls," she said, smiling at both of them. Tears had come to her eyes.

Helen and Anna had taken all of the dried lavender we'd saved from Eastbourne and sewed it up into these little pillows. Everyone received one, to be placed with their clothes. The little sachets would make the house smell nice.

"Oh, thank you, Anna!" I said softly, when my sister handed me a sachet.

As soon as we had all received a pillow, Helen and Anna, beaming happily, sat back down. The now-empty crate sat in the corner while we turned back to our gifts.

"What do you have, Emma?" I asked my elder sister, realizing I had not yet seen her gift from Mum and Father.

She held up a pair of neatly-carved wooden knitting needles. "These. Aren't they lovely? Father did an excellent job carving them." She smiled sweetly at Father.

"And Vi?" Mum looked at me, a question in her eyes.

I had not yet opened my package. I hadn't even glanced at it. I turned my attention to it for the first time that morning. The rectangular-shaped package was wrapped in brown paper. Slowly, I untied the string, then slid the paper off.

Sitting in my lap was a large stack of paper.

178

"Mum? Father? For what am I to use this?"

"I thought that you were in need of paper to write to Lilli," Mum explained.

"Oh." I had forgotten the day that I told Mum I needed paper. And paper was expensive—and so much of it at that. But paper was ordinary. Paper wasn't a pair of finely-carved knitting needles. Paper wasn't a model ship. Paper wasn't a package of paper dolls. Paper was just *commonplace.*

Taking a deep breath, I tried to smile at Mum, although my smile felt a bit off. I went to her, and gave her a tight squeeze.

"Thank you, Mum," I said, my voice somewhat shaky.

"You are most welcome, dear. I hoped that you would like it, seeing how you so love writing to Lillian."

"Yes Mum," I answered weakly. "May I be excused, please? I would like to write a letter to Lilli with this new paper."

"Yes, of course. You may go."

I fled the room as quickly as I could. Dropping the stack of paper on the floor by my bed, I watched the

179

package spill open, a fan of paper spreading on my floor. Ignoring my instinct to pick the paper up, I continued to sob into my pillow.

"It's not fair!" I said to myself. "Why are we here? Everything in America is horrible! Mum's illness, the factory, and now this! Paper? For Christmas? It's just not *fair!*" My sobs took a while to subside, but I made sure to not be too loud, for I did not wish that Mum should hear my weeping over presents.

A wet tongue touched my ear and I turned to see Milky curled up beside me on the bed.

"Shoo!" I said angrily, and he leaped off the bed with an annoyed *meow!*

Something hit my window with a thump. I sat up with a start.

"Psst! Violet!"

Another thump.

Peaking out the window, I peered through the streaky glass to the street below. Someone was calling my name, and throwing snowballs at my window to add emphasis.

"Violet!" It was Ethan.

Of course it was Ethan. He always seemed to show up right when I didn't want to see anyone, much less him. But I couldn't be rude, so I slid the window open and peaked outside.

"Yes?"

"Merry Christmas!" His cheeks were red from the cold, but his eyes were bright and merry.

"Is that all?" My voice was colder than I had intended.

"Violet, what's the matter?"

"I got paper for Christmas." Saying that, without having to smile and act cheerful, felt nice.

"So?"

"Ethan, don't you get it? Paper—for Christmas!"

"I would love to get paper for Christmas. Don't you like to write letters?"

"Yes, but..." I said, struggling in my attempts to explain this to him. "It's just so... so... so ordinary," I finished.

Ethan's face grew solemn. "Paper isn't ordinary. Paper is a blessing. How would you feel if you didn't get anything at all?"

Something in his face was strange when he asked the last question. I wondered if he had received anything for Christmas, and then blushed to think that I was complaining to him about paper, when he may not have gotten anything.

"Ethan, what did you get for Christmas?"

He was silent.

"Didn't you receive anything? Anything from your parents?"

Ethan's dark brown eyes grew fierce.

"My parents are dead, Violet." His voice was flat. "Why do you think I live with my uncle?"

"Oh," I said softly, almost too softly for him to hear. "I'm so sorry."

"You should be!"

"What?" My eyes blazed. "Ethan, I didn't know! Do you blame me for not knowing? You never told me! And now you're acting as though I caused their death!"

"You're right." His face was calmer. "I'm sorry. It's just..."

182

"What happened?" My voice was a whisper, but I knew that he heard me, for his face contorted strangely, as though trying to keep from crying.

"They... they died."

I could barely breathe.

"They died of scarlet fever," he continued, in a voice heavy as lead. "I was only ten years old."

I waited for him to continue.

"We came to America together. But my mum was weak. She wasn't very strong. Father tried to tend to her. We couldn't afford to have the doctor come and look at her. After she passed away, Father succumbed to the sickness as well. My uncle was kind, and he adopted me after my parents' deaths.

"I could have saved them! I could have helped them! But I didn't! And now it's too late."

"No it isn't!" My voice was strong and forceful. "Ethan, it's not your fault they died! You cannot blame yourself! God alone can control life and death. You had no affect on their deaths!" By now I was crying myself, the tears streaming down my face as I spoke.

He lifted his head towards my window. "If I had helped them..."

"No!" I cried, choking on my tears. "No! You are wrong, you are wrong!" I sank to the floor despairingly. What could I say to make him believe me?

Father sighed as he stretched back in his chair. "Dinner was delicious, Kathleen," he said to my mum, squeezing her hand. "I've never had a more delectable ham."

Mum beamed down at Father from her position by the head of the table, where she was standing with a covered basket of biscuits, making sure that everyone had all they needed.

"Oh yes, Mum, it was delicious!" Emma said sweetly. "My ham just melted in my mouth."

"Really?" Helen said quizzically. "My ham didn't dissolve like melted butter. I chewed it, and then I swallowed."

"Oh, no, Helen," Emma giggled. "The phrase 'melted in my mouth' means it was very soft and tender. It didn't really *melt in my mouth.*"

"Oh..." But Helen still looked confused.

"Violet? Are you all right? You've hardly touched your food." Mum looked at me, concerned.

"Oh, I'm fine," I said lightly.

"Are you sure?" Mum asked, her voice full of apprehension.

"Mum, she said she was fine," Helen said, fishing a biscuit off of my untouched plate. "What more is there to it?"

"I suppose," Mum said. But she didn't look very convinced.

Emma stood, her empty plate in her hand.

"You really look pale, Vi," she said. "The ham was delicious—did you not like it?"

"No, no," I said. "The ham was very good."

"How can you tell?" Helen asked. "You have barely eaten two bites!"

"Maybe you should go lie down, dear," Mum said, looking to Father.

"Violet, your mother is right. Go lay down on your bed for a little while."

As I left the room, I heard Mum saying in a low voice, "Do you think she has a fever?"

Once in my room, I flung myself onto my bed and wept bitterly. How could I explain it to Mum? It wasn't something that you went and told everybody, and Ethan has not said that I could go and tell someone else. I felt as though it simply wasn't something I wished to speak of out loud.

I heard footsteps approaching the door.

"Violet?"

I lifted my head from the pillow, looking up into Mum's worried eyes.

"Dear, your father and I have been discussing this in the kitchen for a while, and I think I'd better check if you have a fever."

She placed her hand to my forehead. "You feel cool," Mum said. "A fever is clearly not the problem."

Sitting down on my bed, she looked into my eyes, "But what *is* the problem, Vi?"

186

I had to tell someone. Ethan may never forgive me, but I didn't care. I had to tell *someone.* And who else but my mum?

I sighed, sitting all the way up. "It's Ethan, Mum."

She still looked confused.

"Ethan.... came to the window when I was in here crying, er, I mean *writing* earlier. We struck up a conversation, and somewhere in the middle of it, he told me that..."

"That his parents are dead."

I glanced up at Mum, started. "How... how did you know?"

"Mr. Peterson told me once, when I was up at the shop."

"Oh."

"Is that all you wished to tell me, dear? I feel as though there is something more."

"Yes... there is something more." My voice was low. "Mum, I've never felt this immense sadness before! When you were sick, I felt awful... but you were healed. The Hartleys *didn't* heal... and I didn't get a chance to help them."

187

"Dear, *no one* got a chance. We were not yet in America when they died. It was many years ago."

"But he said he was responsible, Mum! He thought it was his fault! I tried to explain that it wasn't, that he was wrong, but he wouldn't listen." I buried my head into her apron and wept.

Mum stroked my hair softly. "Violet, that's a common occurrence, and Ethan's certainly not the first to feel that way. When I was a young girl, I had a friend— Gloria was her name—who had that same experience. Her mum died, and Gloria felt as though she was responsible for her death. Soon enough, she came to realize that the blame did not lie in her. Ethan will realize the same. It just takes time."

"But what can we do in the meantime, Mum?"

"Wait. That's all we can do. Sooner or later, Ethan will come to the realization that his parents' deaths are *not* his fault. But that won't happen overnight—it will take time. Give it time, Vi."

"But what can *I* do?"

"You can start by praying for Ethan; praying that God will show him that he is not to blame and he should not feel so troubled over this. He needs to learn to let God take his burden away from him. I like Ethan," Mum admitted. "He is a pleasant lad, and very hardworking. But he seems to want to stand on his own two feet too much. There will be times when he cannot always bear his burdens himself. Pray that he will learn to give them to God."

Mum stood, brushed a tear from my cheek, and then left the room.

I knelt by my bed slowly.

"Dear God," I prayed. "Please let Ethan see that he cannot bear this burden alone—that he needs You to take it from him. Please let him come closer to You. He's my friend, God. I hate to have him feeling such pain, with no one to whom he can talk about it. So please take this burden of his, and lift it from his shoulders. And please show me if there is anything else I can do. Amen."

I stood from my kneeling position by the bed, feeling that God had taken my burden too, by providing Mum as a listening ear and a kind, wise heart. I walked across the floor, through the open door, and back to the kitchen.

CHAPTER 17

The next few days were busy, as we cleaned the house back up from the holidays. We swept the floors, for our Christmas tree had dropped many a needle, and these were sprinkled all over the house by Grace and Henry especially. Mum decided that this would be as good a time as any to wash the windows and dust, so our workload was doubled.

Mum paused in her sweeping and sighed. "Grace," she said to my little sister. "No more playing in the needles. I need to sweep them up." Mum turned to me and asked, "Vi, can you take them outside, please?"

"Yes, ma'am," I answered. "Come, Gracie." I took her small hand, then went in search of the others.

Henry was in the kitchen, watching Emma make candles.

"What with all this fat from the ham," Emma commented, "we won't need to buy any store-bought candles this winter."

I nodded, pleased that Mum and Father would be able to save some extra money. "Henry, Mum wants me to take you outside. We can play in the snow, while Mum and Emma get the cleaning done."

"But I'm helping make candles!" Henry objected.

"I'll still have plenty of candles with which you can help me by the time you get back, Henry," Emma said quickly. "Go outside with Vi now."

Henry nodded up at Emma, then ran to get his wraps; he always listened to her.

I sat down at the dining room table, watching Emma dip candles. She held the rod carefully, without shaking, so that the candles would be evenly dipped. Mum always said Emma was good at things such as candle-making, for she had a steady hand, and she was patient.

"You'd best go make sure Henry is getting into his wraps," Emma said, not taking her eyes from the candles she held. "You know how he can get distracted."

192

I smiled, knowing that it was often hard to keep Henry on the same task. "However did you manage to keep him interested for so long?"

"Easy," Emma said, smiling. "I let him help me. Works like a charm."

I had never considered that before.

"You should go, Vi, to make sure he's not playing around."

I nodded, then left the warm kitchen.

I stood watching my siblings play in the snow for a while. Their happy voices rang out in the cold air. I noted with pleasure that Robert was building a large fort, in which Gracie sat, as if she were a princess being guarded by her knight.

Soon my legs grew tired, and I sat down slowly on the step, only to jump back up in an instant. Little had I remembered that the steps were as snowy as the ground. I paused for a moment, looking around to make sure that no one was watching me, and then slowly dusted the snow off the seat of my skirt with my hands. The cold snow went straight through my mittens to my hands, leaving my fingers tingling.

"Helen! Anna!" I called. "I need you to watch Robert, Grace and Henry. I have to go inside and get another pair of mittens."

"Why?" Anna asked.

"Mine are wet. I sat in a snow bank on the steps."

Helen giggled.

"Just watch your siblings, please?" I said. "I'll be but a minute. I just need to grab a dry pair of mittens.

"But I don't..." Helen started to speak.

"Helen, I won't be long. Just stay here until I get back."

Then I turned and ran into the apartment building, up the stairs, and then knocked on the door.

Emma answered, wiping her hands on her apron.

"Violet? Why are you coming in so soon? Where are the others?"

"They're still outside. I sat in a snow bank, and I need a dry pair of mittens," I said, showing her my cold, wet hands. I noticed Milky purring by the warm stove in perfect comfort and envied him.

"Of course," Emma said. "Take those mittens off and lay them by the stove. I'll got get my pair of mittens for you to wear."

"Thank you," I sighed in relief. My cold hands tingled as I held them over the warm stove.

Emma's voice called from the next room:

"Violet, who is watching the children?"

"Helen and Anna were to be doing that."

"Is that quite smart, Vi?" Emma questioned, coming into the room, the dry pair of mittens in her hand. "They are but ten years of age..."

"They'll be fine, Emma," I said quickly, taking the mittens and thrusting my cold hands into them eagerly. "Besides, I'm going back out right now."

"All right," Emma said. "Don't take your eyes from them for a minute."

"I won't," I said, then ran back down the stairs and outside.

Once outside in the bright sunlight, a forlorn scene met me.

"Helen's gone, Vi," Henry said, running to me.

"What?!" I gasped, alarmed. Cold fear trickled down my back. "Anna, what happened?"

Tears shown in her eyes. "As soon as you left, she said that she didn't want to babysit. She said that she didn't want to stay, and then she just ran off."

"I tried to stop her," Robert said, coming towards me, "but she wouldn't listen to me. She said I was just a baby." His eyes shone angrily at the remembrance of this insult.

"Anna, you must stay with Gracie and Henry," I said, trying to keep my voice calm but only half succeeding. "Take them in to Emma and make sure to tell her where we're going."

She nodded, taking Grace and Henry's hands and leading them inside. Grace turned her little face around to stare back at me as Anna led her along.

"Come, Robert," I said briskly, as soon as they were inside. "Let's go."

He understood immediately the direness of the situation, and started walking quickly, calling for Helen.

We stopped first at the butcher shop, but neither Ethan nor Mr. Peterson had seen the missing girl. Mary O' Neale could give no directions as to where she might be, either. Robert ran up and down streets, shouting "Helen!" but the only reply we got were the bewildered stairs from passersby.

We scoured the whole city, calling her name. No one had seen her. In a city like this, Helen could easily have slipped between peddlers stalls without their noticing; she could be anywhere and no one would be able to locate her. We screamed until our throats grew sore and our words hoarse. Not once did she answer back.

I was running out of ideas as to where she could be, but I held firm to the hope that we would find her. I couldn't let myself think that she was gone for good—we had to find her. We simply had no other choice. We would search the city high and low dozens of times if necessary.

Finally Robby and I made it down to the harbor. The chaos made by all the ships coming and going made it nearly impossible to hear or see anything. The salt-

and-fish smell of the harbor stung my nose. Where could Helen *be*?

Suddenly, I noticed a small girl was leaning over the water, a stormy expression on her face. Too late, I realized that it was Helen.

"Helen!" I called, but the wind carried off my voice.

She didn't hear us. I saw her take a step back from the water. Her foot slipped on the icy dock. And suddenly, with a vigorous flailing of arms and legs, she fell into the freezing water with a splash.

"Helen!" I screamed into the cold wind. And before I knew what I was doing, I was running towards the water into which she had fallen. Robert's hand was clutched in my hand, and I was dragging him along with me. When I reached the edge of the dock, I stared into the swirling white foam. Helen was nowhere to be seen.

I didn't want to do it. I could just reach into the water and pull her out. I didn't *have* to jump into the water... or did I? I didn't want to do it—I wouldn't do it! The water was freezing cold, worse than it had been when I had refused to swim in the ocean in Eastbourne

198

with Lilli. But I had no other choice—it was my sister down there. My little emotional sister, Helen. And the longer I delayed, the more her chances of survival lessened.

"Stay here, Robert," I said sternly. "Don't move." And then I dove into the water.

It was much colder than I had expected. The weight of the water pushed down on me and made it hard for me to breathe. My muscles froze and grew stiff, and the contents of my brain seemed to swirl around me like little waves of sea water—just out of my reach. For a moment I couldn't remember why I was in the water and what I was to do. Then it hit me.

Helen. I had to save her. There was nothing else to do.

I pushed against the strong current, which seemed to have a mind of its own. The waves pulled me further out to sea, but I struggled against them, kicking violently. All the while I reached for Helen, but my hands never seemed to find her.

I was getting frantic. Kicking faster and with more violence, I heaved against the water, hating it more than

199

ever at that moment for keeping me from saving my sister.

Finally, I caught one of her curls. Her wet hair slipped past my fingertips and I grabbed at it and yanked. There—I had her! Now we just had to reach the dock.

But that soon proved to be far trickier than we thought. What with the current pushing us further and further out to sea, we were now several yards from the dock. I had thought it was hard swimming against the current when it was just me; now that I had Helen with me, it was exhausting. It seemed to take hours before we finally reached the dock.

Using my last bit of strength, I pulled her to the surface and up onto the dock, where we lay gasping on the planks. I felt as though my body had no strength left in it. We both coughed loudly, spitting up saltwater.

"Helen?" I said finally, after a long silence. "Are you all right?"

"Yes," she sighed softly. "I'm fine."

"Why did you run off when I told you to stay with the others?"

"I didn't want to stay, Vi! I tried to tell you that, but you wouldn't listen. And why did *you* run off?"

"My mittens were wet! I had to get a dry pair." Even as I explained that now, it sounded like a pitiful excuse.

"I suppose," Helen said, sighing again. "But you didn't have to get your mittens wet in the first place! You didn't have to sit down in that snowdrift."

"Do you think I *wanted* to get wet?" I asked incredulously.

"Well... no," Helen said quietly, blushing. "I'm sorry, Violet. I shouldn't have run off."

I pressed my lips to her wet hair, which smelled of the ocean. "It's all right, Helen. I should never have left."

We trudged home slowly, our sodden clothes weighing us down. The freezing, bitter wind made it even more uncomfortable for us in our wet state. The one thing on my mind now was to get home and get Helen and myself into dry clothes.

Mary spotted me from her father's forge, where she was shoveling snow from the walk.

"Violet!" she called to me, dropping her shovel to run towards us. "Vi, why on earth are ye wet?"

"She dove into the harbor," Robby said matter-of-factly. His voice was somewhat stiff through his blue lips.

Mary's eyes widened in shock. "But it's below freezing out there!"

"Yes, well, Helen slipped in first, and so Vi had to jump in and save her." Robby spoke so solemnly that I had to smile.

"Well," Mary said slowly. "It certainly sounds like ye've had quite the adventure. Ye'd best head straight home and git some dry frocks on." She shivered as she said this, rubbing her cold hands together. "Me da will be more than a wee bit frustrated if he sees me standin' 'round a'chattin' when I should be completin' me work." She smiled at me, waved, and then walked back to her task.

I waved back, then led my siblings up the stairs to our apartment, our wet clothes dripping on the stairs.

Milky was the first to welcome our arrival with a loud *meow.*

"They're back, Mum!" Emma called. "Helen, you're soaked through! What happened?" She grabbed a blanket from a cupboard. "Here, come with me, dear. We'll get you a hot bath."

"Oh, girls," Mum said with a sigh. "I was so worried about you." She looked down at Helen, around whom Emma had already wrapped a warm blanket. "Don't you ever run away from your sister again, Helen— you must mind her."

"Yes, ma'am," Helen sighed, face downcast.

"Mum, it wasn't her fault," I interjected. "I am to blame as well. I should not have left them to get mittens. I should have sent Henry in to get me a pair. I'm sorry, Mum. It's my fault she almost drowned today."

"Well," Mum said slowly, her hands on her hips. "I suppose all's well that ends well. You girls get into hot baths now—I don't want anyone sick. Emma, could you help me with the water?"

Emma nodded quickly, then grabbed the metal tub from the shelf above the stove. She helped Mum

203

pump water into the tea kettle, then set it on the stove to boil. When the water was boiling, she poured it into the bucket. After several kettles of water, the tub was finally full enough.

"Come, Helen," she said. "I'll give you your bath first."

"Violet, I want you to come to my room, please," Mum said, when everyone—except for Emma and Helen—had left the kitchen.

I looked questioningly towards Mum, but she simply motioned for me to follow her into her room.

Once in the room, with the door closed, Mum gestured for me to sit on the bed beside her.

"Violet," she said. "I want you to tell me what happened today, not leaving anything out."

I related to her the events of the morning, watching her face closely for any signs that she was angry. When I finished, Mum sighed.

"Violet..." she said slowly. "I thought I could trust my fourteen-year-old daughter to watch the children."

"Yes, Mum, you can—normally," I started to say. "But I sat down on the snowy steps, and then—"

204

Mum interrupted me, "And then, what? You sat down on the snowy steps today. Tomorrow Mary O' Neale may have something important to tell you. Every day you will be faced with situations that will try to pull you from your duties. A letter from Lillian, perhaps, or a friend who wishes to talk. It doesn't matter. You simply cannot leave a task that you are given."

"But Mum, what was I to do?"

"You presented an excellent option in the kitchen just a little while ago, Vi. You said you could have sent Henry in to get the mittens—and I wish you had. Your one wrong choice caused a whole lot of trouble this afternoon."

"Yes, Mum," I said, bowing my head. "I'm so sorry, Mum."

"I know, dear," she said. "And of course I forgive you. I just want you to grow up to be a dependable wife and mother. You are nearly fifteen, after all, and you could be married in but three or four more years. I don't want to send my daughter out not prepared to manage her household, simply because she gets distracted by little things. I want to be proud of you, dear." She stroked my brow, then said, "And most days I am. But today... this accident could have been prevented."

She kissed my forehead. "Go now, dear. Helen must be nearly done in the bath."

CHAPTER 18

"Well, girls," Mum said the next morning at the breakfast table. "I do think we have successfully completed our housework. Everything looks orderly again. I'm so thankful for all of your helping hands."

"Even if those hands were encased in wet mittens," Helen said mischievously, grinning at me.

"Helen..." Mum said warningly, although she too smiled.

"I am very grateful that *all* my beautiful children are safe and well," Father said from his seat at the head of the table. "I don't want to think of what could have happened."

Helen and I both blushed, and suddenly were very busy putting butter on our bread.

Robby looked to Father, an important look on his face. "I helped them," he said. "I went with Vi to find Helen. I helped them home."

"I am very thankful for your help as well, Robert," Father said. "But remember Proverbs chapter sixteen verse eighteen."

"What's that?" Robby asked.

"Pride goes before destruction, a haughty spirit before a fall," Mum quoted solemnly.

Helen snickered under her breath. I gave her a warning look.

"Oh, I understand," Robby said. "If I'm standing on the edge of a cliff, I shouldn't be prideful, because I might fall."

Suddenly, Helen was not the only one giggling.

"Emma, it's almost one month, and I still haven't received a new letter from Lillian. I wonder what's taking her so long?" I said, later that afternoon.

"I don't know, Vi—perhaps she's been delayed by something that happened in Eastbourne."

"Yes, but she hasn't written for one month!" I said. Emma wasn't understanding the direness of this situation. "Something must be terribly wrong."

Before Emma had time to reply, Robert had skidded in through the front door on icy shoes.

"Mail!" he said. "Vi, there's a letter for you."

"Really?" I asked eagerly. "Is it from Lilli?"

"I'm not sure—ah, yes it is." He handed the fat envelope to me.

My fingers tingled with excitement. I ripped the envelope open quickly, letting it fall to the floor, and removed the several pages. I began to read, curious at what had taken my friend so long to write back.

Dearest Vi,

I am so sorry for not writing in such a long time. Things have been quite busy around here, what with the holidays to prepare for—I simply have not had a moment of time to write a letter. But now, dear, you shall get a very long letter.

Father has been very busy in his shop as of late, and we have all been helping out, for the end of the year is always a busy time. He sells certain fine things that cannot be bought anywhere else, and so many a gentleman or lady comes to him to purchase a Christmas gift for a loved one.

Christmas was delightful, Vi. I so wish you could have been here. The church had a wonderful service, and we all attended. I do admit that I don't think I listened to the actual sermon much—I was so distracted by the beautiful decorations, you see. Bows of holly and evergreen were hung everywhere, with big red bows. It was so lovely—it would have taken your breath away, Violet, as it did mine.

After the service on Christmas Eve, we went home. Mum made hot chocolate, and we all sat around the dining room table, discussing the service. As I said before, I didn't listen to the sermon much, so I don't think I contributed much to the conversation. But it was so nice to sit—all cozy with your family—and just talk, for you <u>know</u> I am very good at talking.

Father read the Christmas story from the Bible that night as well. Just think what it must have been like for the shepherds on the night of Jesus' birth, startled out of their skin by the angels. I know I would be very startled if I was sleeping after a long day's work, and suddenly a bright light and a host of angels surrounds me. And what's more, they were singing—"Glory to God in the highest, and on earth peace, good will toward men." Just the very thought of it thrills me to my fingertips.

The next morning, we all woke early, eager to see our stockings. Father was very secretive; he didn't let us downstairs for about an hour, and there was much rustling going on down there. I tried to peak—just to get a glimpse of what was going on—but Will caught me. You know how my older brother is, always trying to play the parent. So I didn't get to see it until Father called and said that everyone

211

could come downstairs. And I'm glad that Will stopped me from seeing, for otherwise the surprise would not be nearly as breathtaking...

We each received a few nice gifts. Father and Mum gave us books and made us several nice pairs of stockings and mittens and scarves. You know we do not have the funds to afford expensive gifts. I was glad to receive anything at all.

The feast we had that night was... oh, words cannot describe it. We had pumpkin bread, vegetables, a goose, numerous jams and jellies, light bread and dark bread, plum pudding, and a ham! A large ham—it was very good! The kind ladies of the church had put their finds together so that they could send us the feast. Oh, it was so kind of them. They were so sweet and generous, thinking of nothing for themselves.

You *did* have a ham, didn't you Violet? If you haven't, I feel very sorry for bringing it up and tempting you. I shall not talk about it

212

anymore, for any pain that my dearest friend Violet feels, that pain I feel as well.

I paused in my reading and laughed at this part of the letter. Sometimes Lilli could be just like Helen!

Well, I have succeeded, I think, in giving you a long letter, Vi. I shall stop now, for I have written long enough. Mum will be needing my help with chores.

Love,

Lillian

P.S. One last thing: could you pray that my brother will get another job? He used to work with the lifeboat makers, and they had a large order of lifeboats needed for the Titanic. Suddenly, they received word that the Titanic doesn't need the lifeboats—and so they don't need Will's help anymore. He's out of a job now, and his income was a great help to our family.

"Well," I said, after having read the letter aloud to my family, "Lilli certainly can be long-winded when she wants to be."

"Long-winded?!" Henry sputtered. "That letter took hours to read! It must be nearly Christmas 1912 by now!"

I grinned at his impatience.

"No, not Christmas," Mum said. "But it *is* nearly supper time, and I have yet to get the table set. Henry, would you do the honors please?"

"Yes, ma'am!" Henry said, saluting like a soldier.

Mum smiled at him, then turned to the stove.

"I think the ham bone we had left over from the holidays will be very flavorful in this soup," she said, stirring the soup.

"Ham in soup?" Grace asked.

"Not ham in soup," Emma corrected. "The ham *bone* is in the soup."

"We're going to eat a *bone*?!" Anna asked in alarm.

"No, no," I said. "Mum put the bone in there to make it more flavorful. We're not going to eat the bone."

"Oh, good," Anna said in relief.

"So we're not eating the bone?" Grace asked.

"No, Gracie, don't worry—we're not eating the bone," I said to her.

"Aw..." she said. "I wanted to see what a bone tasted like."

CHAPTER 19

I saw Ethan at the butcher's a week later. I felt awkward and uncomfortable after our discussion on Christmas morning about his parents' deaths, and so I walked quickly into the store, bought what a needed, and then left, head down. I would have succeeded in getting away quickly if he hadn't stopped me.

"Violet, wait!" He grabbed my arm.

"Ethan, I really wish you had a more pleasant way of getting my attention," I said crossly, pulling my arm away.

"Sorry, Violet. I'm so sorry."

This sounded like it was about more than my arm. "Ethan, what is it?" I asked, my voice a bit softer.

"It's you, really."

My face went pale. What did he mean?

"I've been thinking about what you said to me—how only God can control life and death, and how you think I shouldn't blame myself for my parents' deaths."

"Yes..." I wasn't sure where he was going.

"And I suddenly felt as though God had laid it upon my heart this week—I kept thinking of what you said to me. You were so adamant, but I refused to listen to you. I'm so sorry, Violet. And you were right."

"So you mean..."

"I now know that I was not to blame for their deaths."

"How on earth did this come about?" I asked in shock.

"Well, it certainly didn't happen overnight. I can be stubborn—I know that well enough. I wasn't about to admit that you were right—I didn't *want* you to be right. I've lived my whole life since my parents' deaths thinking that I was to blame, and I wasn't about to let you shake my whole world to pieces. Now, don't get me wrong—I didn't *enjoy* blaming myself. But I was *someone* to blame. I wanted a reason for their deaths, and I found that reason in myself.

217

"I was stubborn, and I didn't want to change," he admitted. "But little by little, I felt my resolve melting. I tried to build it back up again; I tried to relive the pain and heartache, only to discover that it was gone. I no longer felt guilty for their deaths. I felt as though a huge burden had been lifted from my shoulders, a burden I had subconsciously been carrying for years. All thanks to you."

"Oh no, Ethan," I said. "No thanks to me—thanks to Him. He has answered my prayers!"

"Your prayers?"

"I prayed about this, Ethan. I didn't know what to say to you, so empty and desolate did you look. So... I told my mum. I'm really sorry, but I had to tell *someone*, and I know she won't ever tell a soul, if that's what you want. Anyway, she suggested that I pray about it—that I pray that God would change your heart, and help you see that you are not to blame. And He has answered my prayers!"

I went home and told Mum straightaway. She was the one who had encouraged me to pray for Ethan in the first place, after all—she deserved to know.

218

"Oh, Violet, you don't know how happy I am," she said. "There's nothing worse than a human being who thinks he or she is to blame for a friend or family members' death. It's such a relief to hear this news, dear."

"Have you been praying too, Mum?"

"I have, dear. Your father has as well."

"You told him? But Mum..."

"But what, dear? Your father is my husband. I love him very much, and so I tell him these things. You will understand one day when you are wed. Wives are not to keep anything from their husbands—'the two shall become one.'"

"But do you think Ethan will... mind?"

"I can't say. But he doesn't necessarily have to know. When you told him that you told me, I think he naturally expected me to tell your father. That's the way things work, dear."

"Will I really understand when I am married, Mum?"

"You will, dear. Of that I am certain."

Violets Are Blue

Milky was now full-grown. Grace loved to carry him around in her arms, like a baby, though I don't think he enjoyed it much. But as a whole, he was becoming quite the pleasant cat to have around the apartment. I loved stroking his sleek back, whenever he would sit still long enough.

On this particular afternoon, Milky was purring in the corner contentedly. Mum was outside, getting the milk from the milkman, and Emma was teaching Grace how to knit. Helen and Anna were by now excellent knitters, and they were sitting at the table, eyes lit up with eagerness as I slowly taught them how to purl. This knitting technique was a bit more difficult than the basic knitting stitch, and soon Helen threw down her needles in frustration.

"I'll never get it!" she said.

"It's easy, Helen. Come sit down and try again," I coaxed her.

"Yes, it's very easy," Anna added. She was already purling beautifully.

"Easy for you to say!" Helen said. "Everything I do, you always do it better!"

"Oh Helen, that's not true," Emma spoke up from across the room. "You are an excellent knitter—just as good as Anna. If you sit down and learn patiently, you will soon catch on."

"I don't want to sit down and do it!" Helen said. "I'll play with Milky." She walked over to the cat and started to pick him up.

"Helen, no! He's sleeping—he'll scratch you!"

"No he won't," she insisted. "Come Milky, would you like to play?"

The cat woke up with a start, and his eyes were startled from being awoken out of a deep slumber. Seeing the balls of yarn on the floor, he pounced on them, swiftly tangling himself up.

"Oh, Helen!" Emma said. "Look what you did!"

Milky lifted his head and meowed pitifully, for he didn't enjoy being trapped.

"What?" Helen asked. "I guess he didn't want to play."

"What will Mum say? You've wasted a lot of yarn, Helen," Anna said reproachfully.

Just then Mum entered with the milk cans. "What happened?" she asked in surprise.

"Milky likes yarn," Anna said solemnly.

"Most cats do," Mum replied. "I was referring to the fact that I now am short one ball of yarn. How did this happen, girls?"

"Helen was tired of knitting, so she woke Milky up when he was sleeping—she wanted to play with him—and well... I'm sure the rest is obvious."

"Very obvious," Mum said. Her face looked stern, but the corners of her mouth looked like they were struggling to stay downturned. "Well, I suppose we shall have to buy more yarn, girls. I don't want this to happen again, do you understand? We can't afford to waste yarn like this. Helen, you now know not to wake Milky up when he is sleeping."

"Yes, Mum," Helen said solemnly.

"Cats don't like being awakened from their sleep," Mum said. "Especially by very eager little girls."

I saw Ethan again the next afternoon. I was at the post office, mailing my letter to Lilli. He had a letter in his hand, too—I wondered to whom he was writing.

"Violet!" he said, coming towards me.

I smiled in greeting, then asked him about his letter.

"Oh, well... I had many good mates back in England, and I still like to write to them, just a line here and there, to tell 'em how I'm doing."

"Ah," I said slowly, my curiosity still not satisfied. "Did you have many mates in England?"

"No..." he said slowly. "I was so dedicated to helping me parents with the chores—being a responsible son, you see—and they teased me for that. All they wanted was to play around, and I didn't want to do that with them. There were a few lads who were my very good friends. I still write to them now and again."

"That's nice," I said. Then, more hesitantly, "Ethan, what happened with your parents?"

I waited for him to grow angry, sad—any emotion other than calm. But he stood before me, still quiet.

"Why are you so curious about them, Violet?" he asked simply.

I shrugged. "I don't know... maybe I just think that, since we're friends, I might be able to help you by knowing."

"You've already helped me."

"Yes, but I want to do more! I want to feel as though I was there, so I can *understand.* I hate feeling as though this is a huge barrier."

"All right, Violet. I'll tell you," he answered.

"I was born in Yorkshire. We lived on the moors— we weren't the fine city folk my uncle and I are now." He grinned at me at this last part, for he lived in a small apartment with his uncle and aunt, no bigger than my apartment.

"Well," he continued. "We wanted a better life. My uncle and aunt had moved to America, and we wished to move to America as well and perhaps reunite with them. We packed up, I said farewell to my good mates, and then we left.

"Didn't you have any siblings?"

"I had a brother—Joseph was his name—but he went missing about a year before we left. To this day I don't know where he went or why he left." Ethan shook his head sadly.

"I'm so sorry," I said softly. I didn't know what else to say.

"Do you want me to continue?"

"Yes, please."

"Well, all went well until we were on board the ship. That's where Mum caught the fever. She tossed and turned for hours, and there was little even the ship's doctor could do for her. I was so worried for her. But we made it to New York City, safe and sound—mostly.

"Once in America, Mum began to get sick again. The scarlet fever returned, but much stronger this time. We couldn't afford to send for the doctor, as I said to you before, and so Father and I had to do the best we could be ourselves. We tried to contact my uncle, but we didn't know where they lived. I hated to see her die. It was the most horrible time of my life.

"After Mum, it didn't take Father long to die as well. He had been getting sick—and growing weak— during the time that we were caring for my mum. I wasn't surprised when he died a week later.

"I was left alone in the world, with no one I knew and no one to care for me. I was in the street one day, buying a loaf of bread—Father had taught me to do that and saved enough money for me to survive for a little while—when I met my uncle. I was so overjoyed to see him, for I was tired of living alone, cold and hungry, by myself. He took me into his home. And I still live there today."

I stood, speechless, on the sidewalk, to which we had gradually walked while Ethan was telling his story. "How... how old were you when this happened?" I asked finally.

"I was but ten years old. It was six years ago."

"It's amazing how generous your uncle was," I marveled. "I mean, who wouldn't take his nephew in, especially if he's all alone? But to keep you—and provide for you—all this time..."

"Are you implying that I'm annoying to have around?" he asked mischievously.

"No, no! I simply meant that... well, he's treated you like his own son."

"That's what my mum wanted for me. She asked before we came that, should anything happen to her and my father, he would take me in. And he kept his promise." Ethan's brown eyes were serious. "He's kept his promise all this time."

There was a moment of silence, for we both were wrapped up in our thoughts. I was pondering all that he had just said to me.

"Didn't you say once that your friend is coming to America?" Ethan asked suddenly.

"I believe I mentioned it once or twice," I replied lightly.

"On what ship will she and her family be sailing?"

"The Prescotts are coming on the *Titanic*. I am almost envious of her, for it is the grandest ship ever made, they say." I paused for a second. "Why?"

"Because my uncle is to sail on that same ship!"

"Your uncle?" I was confused. "Ethan, your uncle is already here. What do you mean by saying that he is sailing on the *Titanic* as well?"

"No, no, not Uncle George," Ethan explained, laughing. "He's my mother's brother. My father's brother, my Uncle Wallace, is a musician. He's to be the bandleader on the *Titanic*."

"Really?" I asked in amazement. "That's incredible."

"Perhaps Lilli will meet Uncle Wallace on the ship," he said.

"I don't think that's likely to happen," I replied. "Lilli will be staying in the third class quarters, you see. Will your uncle be staying in first class?"

"Second class," Ethan corrected me. "He wasn't hired by the White Star Line. He and the rest of the band are employed by Messrs. C.W. and F.N. Black of Liverpool."

"Think of the honor of being the band of the grandest ship in the world," I said almost dreamily.

"Oh, they're not the only band," he told me. "Uncle Wallace and his quintet are to play at teatime, after dinner, and for the Sunday service. There's another band that plays in the reception room outside the two restaurants."

"Oh," I said, blushing slightly at my mistake. "Well, I'd better go, Ethan. There are no letters here for me, and Mum will be anxious if I am out too long." Waving goodbye quickly, I turned and made my way back to the apartment.

CHAPTER 20

Upon arriving home from a short walk one day, I was surprised to see Mrs. Woods in the kitchen, sipping tea and chatting with Mum.

"Mrs. Woods!" I gasped, running into the room, just barely remembering to drop a curtsy.

"Ah Violet, you've not changed a bit, have ya?" Mrs. Woods laughed. She was holding baby Abby in her arms.

"I invited her over to have tea, Violet," Mum said. "I hadn't gotten a chance to see Abby yet, after all."

"How are you, Mrs. Woods?" I asked politely.

"Mighty fine, Miss Violet," she answered, rocking her baby. "Abby's been growin' so quick, I can't hardly keep track. I don't want her to grow up too fast, after all—seems like she was just born yesterday. But I guess some things ya just can't control."

"No, ma'am," I said.

"All my little ones were like that," Mum said softly. "I never wanted them to grow up. With Grace, especially, it has been very hard to watch her grow up, for she's my last little baby."

"Ah, yes, it must have been very hard," Mrs. Woods said understandingly. "Abby here is the result of much prayer. I couldn't have children for the longest time."

"Will you have more?" I asked curiously, forgetting my manners.

"Only if it is God's will," Mrs. Woods replied. "I can't know His plan—all I can do is follow it. But I would love to have some more children." She then turned to Mum, and said, "How old is your eldest?"

"She will be seventeen this coming summer," Mum said.

"She could be married and havin' babies in just a few years!" Mrs. Woods said. "No, Mrs. Bradshaw, you will never be at a loss for babies."

I smiled at Mrs. Woods' words, imagining my sister as a busy wife with five children. She was a wonderful helper around the apartment—she would be an excellent mother.

"Well, I'd best be getting home," Mrs. Woods sighed, rising from her chair. "Mr. Woods will be wantin' his supper. Lovely to chat with you, Mrs. Bradshaw," she added, smiling towards Mum. "You too, Violet. Be sure to come and visit me once in a while."

"I will, ma'am," I said. "Thank you for coming."

"Good evenin'," she said in farewell, then left.

"Well, Vi, will you help me with supper?" Mum asked. "Mrs. Woods' visit had put me a bit behind in my preparing. I planned on making corn pudding, but the time has run out. Please get the bread from the cupboard."

"Yes, Mum," I said, taking the loaf down from its shelf.

"Mum?" I said a moment later, while I sliced the bread, "did you ever have this feeling... that something terrible was going to happen?"

"Like what, dear?"

"I'm not sure," I said. "We're all well, we have good food, Father's business is prospering... nothing is
232

wrong. And yet I feel this weight upon me like something awful is going to occur."

"Don't worry too much about your own feelings, Violet," Mum said. "We don't want to be guided by our emotions."

"I know, Mum, of course," I answered quickly. "It's just so... odd. I thought I was feeling sad because of Ethan's parents, but that's not a problem anymore. It's like something is wrong and I just can't put my finger on it."

"Most likely you are analyzing your feelings and emotions too much, dear," Mum said lightly. "It's no use wasting your time over something that is simply nonexistent. Now go call your siblings to the table."

I tried to tell myself that Mum was right and that I was being silly and foolish. But that nagging feeling didn't go away.

I wrote a long letter to Lillian that night, staying up far later than I should have, in order to finish it. I'd always hated to make Lilli wait long for a letter.

Dear Lillian,

Much has happened here in New York as of late. Helen nearly drowned, although how this came about will take much telling. I will tell about that later; for now, let me assure you that we had both a ham and a Christmas tree for Christmas, so you needn't worry. We enjoyed both, although the ham tasted quite a bit better than the Christmas tree would have.

Now, about Helen. I was told to watch the children outside, for Mum and Emma were inside doing housework. There was much cleaning to be done after the holidays, which Mum and Emma wished to accomplish, and being that the children—Grace especially—were

234

getting rather restless, Mum thought it a good idea that I take them out for a breath of fresh air, and so they could run around a bit.

Well, I sat down in a snow bank outside (don't laugh, Lillian Joy Prescott!) and had to use my mittens to brush the snow off my coat. I instructed Helen and Anna to watch the little ones while I was inside, getting new mittens. I know I really shouldn't have done that, but my fingers were freezing, and I was eager to get dry mittens, so I wasn't thinking clearly. I should have asked Anna to run inside, while I stayed outside to watch the children, as Mum asked me. If I was wiser, I would have noticed how against babysitting Helen was at the moment.

As soon as I was inside, I seemed to melt in the warmth of the apartment. Emma ran and got me her pair of mittens to wear, while I sat at the table, just relaxing in the warmth. Emma soon reminded me that the children were outside with only two ten-year-olds to watch them, and I soon ran back outside... only to realize that one of my siblings was gone!

Anna and Henry informed me that Helen had grown restless, and had not wanted to babysit. She ran off, they said, but they didn't know to where she had run. Not wishing to make the same mistake twice, I promptly told

Anna to take Gracie and Henry inside. I took Robert with me, for he is a strong and fast runner, and together we scoured the city, calling for Helen until our throats grew sore. She never answered our calls.

Finally, we made it to the harbor, where I saw Helen. I screamed her name, but the wind carried my words away from me. Helen was leaning over the harbor—far too close for my comfort—and was staring into the dark waters. Well, the inevitable happened soon enough. Helen slipped on ice and fell right into the water. Screaming for Robby to back up and be careful, I dove into the water after my little sister.

The water was so cold, Lilli. It seemed to weigh down on me, making it nearly impossible for me to breathe. You couldn't even imagine it.

Helen was sinking below the surface faster than I could swim in those freezing depths. I grabbed for her once and missed. I grabbed for her again, and this time caught her hair. It took every ounce of my strength, but I pulled us both to the dock. We both lay there, gasping and trying to catch our breath.

I took Helen and Robby home, where Mum was waiting to scold me. I told her of our adventure, and she looked at me sadly, the expression in her eyes unfathomable. Later,

238

when Emma was giving Helen a hot bath, Mum informed me that she was disappointed. I should know better, she said, than to leave my siblings outside alone, especially when I have been strictly directed to take them outside and watch them. She was very upset with me, Lilli, and of that whole day, that was the worst part. I hate disappointing my mother.

There, now you have heard my tale. Do write back soon, Lilli—I long to hear from you. I am growing used to New York, but I still ache for Eastbourne at times. Some things never change, I guess.

Love,

Violet

P. S. Make sure to include any more news you have of the Titanic, and when you shall be departing. I am longing for the day when we shall see each other once more! And just think how lucky you are to be traveling on the largest and most luxurious ship in the world! Oh dear, I fear I shall grow envious of you. You must make sure to write me while you are at sea, not leaving out any details.

I looked at my letter with satisfaction. It was well-written and quite long. I was pleased, for I knew how delightful it is to receive a long letter, and so I enjoyed sending long letters myself. Besides, they made the envelopes look so nice and plump.

After writing my letter, I leaned over and blew out my candle. Emma had been asleep for nearly an hour

240

now, as had all the rest of my siblings. I burrowed under my blankets, trying to get warm.

I was just falling asleep when I heard someone whisper my name. "Violet?"

I opened my eyes instantly and saw Henry's face only a few inches from mine.

"What is it, Henry?" I asked, somewhat impatiently, for I wished to go to sleep.

"I can't sleep."

I sighed. "Why don't you sleep here with me for the rest of the night, Henry," I said, sitting up.

"Alright!" he said eagerly, a grin on his face. I moved over to give him room, trying not to awaken Emma.

"Now go to sleep," I said, as soon as he was comfortable.

"All right..." he answered, rolling over.

I closed my eyes, trying to fall asleep, but Henry's interruption had rendered me sleepless.

"Vi?" my little brother asked questioningly. "Do you think Mum will make a jam roll tomorrow?"

"I don't know," I said, rolling over to face him. "Why do you ask?"

"Well, she has some preserves that she's saved from Eastbourne, and I saw her take them down the other day."

"That proves nothing. What if she wanted to have it with bread for tea?"

"No, no, Violet! I know she was planning on making a jam roll. She makes us use butter on our bread, for we can't get near as nice preserves here as we could in Eastbourne. Why would she suddenly decide put *jam* on her bread?"

"Alright then," I answered quickly. "We now know that there is a slight possibility that Mum will make jam rolls tomorrow. Now please go to sleep, Henry."

He closed his eyes slowly, but soon had opened them again. "Violet?"

"What?" I snapped. It was nearly eleven o' clock by now. He should have been asleep almost three hours ago.

"I was just wondering if you were asleep..." Henry said slowly.

242

"Henry James Bradshaw," I said briskly. "It is almost eleven o' clock at night. I don't think Mum or Father would be very happy to know you are still awake. All the questions you wish to ask me will have to wait for the morning. Now go to sleep."

After that, he promptly closed his eyes and fell asleep.

"Good," I sighed. "Now I can get some sleep." But sleep would not come. I tossed and turned, but it was nearly impossible to feel tired anymore. Finally, at about twelve o' clock, I fell into a restless slumber.

"Violet, you look tired. Did you sleep well last night?" Mum asked the next morning. She looked worried.

I didn't reply, but laughed.

"What is it, Vi?" Emma asked curiously.

Laughing again, I related to them all that had happened the previous night. Mum and Emma smiled at Henry's antics.

"Why is everybody laughing?" Anna asked, coming into the room. She held a brush in her hand, and was still brushing her hair.

"I know why everyone's laughing," Helen said. "Henry kept Violet up really late last night with all of his questions."

"What's wrong with that?" Henry asked, frowning.

"I enjoy answering your questions, Henry," I said. "I really do. Just please don't ask them at eleven o' clock at night!"

"Alright..." Henry sighed, his eyes downcast. But it didn't take long for his eyes to light up with excitement as he saw Mum remove a jam roll from the oven.

Mum was in need of a new pot, and so she sent me to Mr. O' Neale's forge to buy one that afternoon. I was glad to go on the errand, for the blacksmith and I were good friends.

"Yer in luck, Vi," he said, when I asked for the pot. "I've got jist one pot left. Here ye go." He handed me the pot, wrapped up in brown paper. "Do yer sisters and brothers go to school?" he asked, while stoking the fire.

"No; Mum teaches them at home. She doesn't approve of the schools here, and she considers it easier and much more rewarding to teach us herself."

"Ah, yer mam sounds like a mighty busy woman," Mr. O' Neale said. "Do ye ever help her out?"

"Yes, I help her a lot," I said quickly. "But Emma is more of the housekeeper type than I. I am normally sent outside to mind the children."

"I see," Mr. O' Neale answered slowly. "But ye know, Vi, ye might want to get more acquainted with housewifery. Otherwise, ye'll be at a bit o' a loss when it's yer time to marry. Although, caring for children is good practice as well." He scratched his balding head. "Ah me, I don't know what to tell ye. Ye jist keep listenin' to yer mam and followin' her instructions, and ye'll do jist fine."

"I will," I promised.

"What's this I've been hearin' about some little girl fallin' into the harbor a couple weeks back?"

"Oh," I said. I looked down, blushing.

"Was that one o' yer sisters?"

"Yes... it was Helen. My headstrong little sister." And I quickly related to him all that had happened that day.

"Saints preserve us! She could've drowned, Vi! Ye must keep a better eye on yer sisters and brothers."

"I know, I know, Mum told me the same."

"Well, ye'd best be a'gettin' home—yer mam will be a'lookin' for ye. Have a good day, Violet."

"You too, Mr. O' Neale," I said, leaving the forge.

CHAPTER 21

Spring was coming. I could see the signs of it everywhere. The snow was melting, and the air was no longer so cold. Flowers were blooming, and I spent every moment that I could outside. Spring always made me feel so blessed to be alive so that I could experience such beauty.

Spring was also the season in which my birthday took place. The twenty-sixth of March was my birthday; this year I would be fifteen. I knew we had no money for surprises, and so I didn't expect any. But there is some special magic about birthdays, and just thinking about mine coming up made me happy and excited.

"Ouch!" I jumped as the sharp needle pricked my finger. I was sitting in the kitchen, doing the mending, waiting for Father to come home. Emma had taken the children to the Woods', to see Abby, and Mum was in the bedroom changing the bed sheets.

I had never liked sewing much, in any form; I definitely preferred knitting. But Mum insisted that I sew a little every day, for she wanted me to be as proficient a sewer as I was a knitter. I wrapped a small bandage around my pricked finger, thinking of all the reasons for sewing to be banned.

"Hello, Vi," Father said, entering the room at that moment.

"Father!" I ran to give him a hug, my skirt sweeping the stocking I had been mending onto the floor.

"Where are the others?" he asked me, looking around the apartment.

"Emma took the twins, Henry, Gracie, and Robert to see Abby Woods—"

"She's old enough to receive callers?"

"No, Father! You know she's but a few months old. They're going to visit with Mrs. Woods, mainly."

"Ah. And where is your mother?"

"She's in the bedroom," I said, pointing.

"Well then, I'd best go say hello to her as well," Father said. He left the room.

248

I picked the stocking up once more, but I had barely sewn a stitch before a knock sounded on the door. Happy to have an excuse to lay down my needle, I went to the door.

Emma stood at the door, the rest of the children surrounding her.

"Mrs. Woods wanted to feed Abby, so I decided that it was a good time for us to return home," she explained.

"Oh, that's fine," I said, ushering them into the apartment.

"It's no trouble, do you think?" she asked cautiously. "I know that you wished to complete your mending."

"No, it's no trouble, Emma, really," I said. "I'll finish it another day."

"Mind you, just because Emma entered at an odd time does not mean that you don't have to complete your mending, Vi," Mum said. She had just entered the room and caught my last words.

"Of course not, Mum," I said, blushing. I had hoped to get away with pushing the mending off, but it seemed Mum was not going to allow that.

"Violet, you'd best go to your room to complete your mending now, with no distractions," Mum said suddenly. "Take your time, and do it all neatly. I want you to finish mending everything in that basket."

"But Mum, I'm perfectly fine here—"

"No, you are not. No one can sew in such a crowded kitchen without making mistakes, especially when one is as prone to getting distracted as you."

"Yes, ma'am," I said slowly. My feet dragged as I trudged to the bedroom, the mending clenched in my hand.

"And don't get distracted by a book!" Mum called after me.

I closed the bedroom door and sat down on my bed. Seeing no way out of it, I bent over the piles of clothing, intent on finishing this chore. The sooner it was done, the sooner I could do something else.

"Mum! I'm finished!" I called. I heard a scurrying in the kitchen, and the sound of loud pans clanging, as though someone wished to create a diversion. I started to enter, but was soon stopped by Emma's voice:

"Oh Vi, would you mind taking Grace to get her hands washed for supper?"

"All right," I replied. "Where is Grace?"

"Right here," Emma said, emerging from the other bedroom. She had Gracie on her hip. "Take her to get her hands washed, please, and make sure that she doesn't waste water."

"I know, I know." I took Grace from Emma. "Where's Mum and the others?"

"I'm not sure..." my sister answered vaguely. She seemed to know more about the situation than she would admit. "Perhaps they are still completing the preparations for dinner. I'd best go assist them with that."

She left the room quickly. Suddenly I realized something.

"Oh Emma, why couldn't you wash Grace's hands? You were nearer to the washbasin."

No reply.

Still confused, I took Grace's hand and led her back to the bedroom, to the washstand. It didn't take long to rub soap on her hands, scrub them, rinse them clean, and dry them. Soon, I was entering the kitchen again, when another voice called me:

"Vi, would you mind going to the store? We need thread."

"Very well," I answered.

My foot was set towards the kitchen when I heard Helen start to say, "No, not..." and then broke off suddenly, as though a hand had been clamped over her mouth.

Then Mum's voice was saying, "As a matter of fact, I don't need any thread. Why don't you take Grace back to the bedroom? We'll call you when dinner is ready."

Now I knew something was going on, something which everyone refused to tell me. Why were they all so secretive? The fact that it was the twenty fifth of March—tomorrow was my birthday—never occurred to me as the reason behind all of their strange behavior. I simply wondered why they insisted on keeping me from the kitchen. I almost wanted to walk boldly into the kitchen and see what was going on, but I knew that would ruin whatever surprise they were planning.

"Violet, I just got the mail, and there was a letter for you," Emma said. She handed me the envelope.

Forgetting my frustration over whatever they were planning in the kitchen, I immediately opened the letter, unfolding the pages.

Dear Violet,

I was so sorry to hear about Helen, especially since she is one of my favorites of your siblings. I know it is rude to have favorites, but I can't help it—Helen and I seem to have this <u>understanding</u> that none of your other siblings have with me... except for you, of course.

Lilli was entirely right in saying this—she and Helen were practically twins, or so it seemed at times.

Oh, it is less than a month until our great voyage. Every time I think of it, the butterflies come into my stomach. Butterflies of excitement, that is; I am not at all nervous about this sea-crossing. They say she—the Titanic, that is—is so smooth that one does not even know he or she is on a ship. It is more like a floating house!

Would it not be splendid if you were on the ship with me? We could have the most wonderful of times! It would be wonderful. Alas, for you are not in need of a crossing, nor are you here in Eastbourne. Many the time I have wished you could be here, and crossing the ocean with my family, but that cannot be. I must be content that at least I am able to experience it, and then I shall tell you all about it when I return.

We go to Southampton a few days before the ship leaves. Mum insisted upon this, for if there are any delays in our travel, we do not wish to arrive too late. I do not mind, for this means that I will have more time to see the city in the days before our departure.

I should go; Mum is calling me to clean up my art supplies. They are on the table, and I went from them to write a letter to you. I really must learn to finish one task before I start another, Mum always says. I think she's right.

Love,

Lillian

I closed the letter and place it neatly in the envelope. I was just about to write my reply when Henry came to the door.

"Vi, dinner's ready," he said solemnly.

Sighing, I put my writing supplies away and followed him out of the room. It seemed that when I wanted to come into the kitchen, I was not allowed, but when I finally got settled with a task I enjoyed, they wanted me in the kitchen. It was extremely trying.

"Hello, Vi," Mum said calmly. She was placing plates of chicken and vegetables on the table. "Did you complete your mending?"

"Yes Mum, I did," I answered slowly, looking about in confusion. Nothing was amiss in the kitchen; in fact, everything was neat and clean... and normal.

"Mum, what were you doing in the kitchen?"

"Why, preparing supper. Why do you ask?" Mum asked. She looked confused.

"Well... because you were so secretive... and you wouldn't let me enter the kitchen..."

"What are you talking about, Vi? We did not purposely keep you from the kitchen. We simply found that it was easier to complete our supper preparations without Grace in the room. Now, supper is ready, so come and eat."

Mum did not seem willing to admit to whatever she had been doing, and I realized that I must drop the subject, for I was not getting anywhere. I sat down at my seat at the table silently.

Elizabeth Rose

Father said the blessing, and then we all began to eat our stew.

The rest of the evening passed pleasantly. I helped Mum wash the supper dishes, and then we all gathered in Mum and Father's bedroom to read together. I lay across Mum and Father's bed, writing my reply to Lillian's letter:

Oh, Lilli, if you think you are excited, you have no idea how thrilled I am. I cannot wait to see you, to be able to talk to you in person once more. I feel filled with an abundance of joy. This has had a sad affect on my chores, I'll admit, for I don't often complete them in the neatest manner, due to my excitement. I am a great trial to Mum, I

257

think, and yet she knows so well how happy I am, and so she does not scold as much.

Lilli, something rather... odd happened this evening. I was at home with Mum (Emma had taken the children to the 'Woods'), doing the mending. Father arrived home and, after saying hello to me, went to greet Mum as well. Then Emma and the children came home. All was normal until Mum asked me to complete the mending from the confines of my bedroom.

I protested that I was able enough to sew in the kitchen without getting distracted, but she would not hear a word of it. She didn't want me in the kitchen—I could tell. It was strange; almost like she was trying to get rid of me.

Well, I completed the mending (oh, what a tiresome chore!), folded the clothing neatly, and placed it back in the mending basket. I started to enter the kitchen when Emma emerged from Mum and Father's room, asking me to wash Grace's hands for supper. I normally do not mind doing this—in fact, I enjoy my littlest sister's company very much—but today, it was more proof that they wanted to keep me from entering the kitchen. I washed Gracie's hands quickly, then was about to enter the kitchen when I was, yet again, stopped. Mum's voice, coming, strangely enough, from

259

beneath the kitchen table, called me and stopped me in my tracks.

She wished that I should go to the store, to purchase thread. I saw this as only another excuse to keep me out of the kitchen—out of the house, even—so that they could complete whatever it was that they were doing. Besides, I had just been doing the mending, and I knew very well that we were not out of thread!

As I started to leave the apartment, they suddenly seemed to realize that I would need to go through the kitchen to be able to depart. I heard Helen's voice: "No, not—" and then she was cut off, as if someone had just clamped a hand over her mouth to keep her from saying anything more. Then I heard Mum's voice, informing me that she realized we did not need thread. Now, how could she have determined that, if I was just now holding the mending basket? It was all quite confusing.

Mum asked me to remain in my room and keep Gracie occupied until supper was ready. I had half a mind to enter the kitchen— even if force was needed—but realized that would not be fair or right. So, I remained in my room, playing with Grace, until they allowed me to come out.

When I finally entered the kitchen, all was completely normal. Nothing looked strange, odd, or even out of place. Every dish, cup, and bowl was in its place.

I still do not know up to what they have been, nor why it is such a secret. I shall write you if I discover the method to their madness.

Love,

Violet

"Violet," Mum whispered. "It's time to go to bed."

I jumped a little, then looked about me. I realized that everyone had gone to bed. The clock on the wall read ten o' clock. Goodness, it was late. I had not realized how fast the time had flown.

"Goodnight, Mum," I said, giving her a light kiss on the cheek. "Goodnight, Father," I called to him.

"Goodnight, Vi," Father said to me, looking up from his newspaper.

Ten minutes later, I was in my bed, already falling asleep, but still curious about the mysterious happenings earlier today.

"Violet! Violet!" A whispered voice pulled me from my slumber. "Violet!" it called again, this time with much more force. I felt someone gently shake my shoulder.

"What?" I asked, my eyes opening slowly. I squinted in the bright morning light. My whole family was leaning over me, large smiles on their faces. Emma held a plate of steaming French toast, laden with melting butter and syrup—my favorite breakfast choice. Helen and Anna were grinning, their hair combed and neatly braided in identical plaits, holding a large box between them. Grace held another package and Mum held another. Robert held yet another package in his hand as well.

"Surprise!" they all said in unison, and then, "Happy birthday, Violet!"

"Oh..." I whispered. I didn't know what to say; never in my wildest dreams had I expected such a lovely surprise.

"We thought we'd all have breakfast in here together—not to make it a daily occurrence, but just to celebrate your birthday, dear," Mum said.

"That sounds wonderful," I said. The French toast smelled amazing.

"Can we eat?" Helen asked, looking longingly towards the platter in Emma's hand.

"Of course," Mum said. "Here children, let's sit on the floor. Violet can have the seat of honor—the bed—since it is her birthday."

Soon we were all enjoying a lovely breakfast picnic. The French toast was extremely delicious—not for nothing was it my favorite breakfast food.

"Can Vi open her presents now?" Henry asked impatiently, when we all had finished eating.

"Yes, she can," Mum said.

"Here," Grace said, wiping her sticky face with the back of her hand. She pushed her package into my hands. "Open mine first!"

264

"All right, Grace," I answered. Inside the package lay a picture she had drawn for me and a lemon-flavored stick of candy.

"Thank you, Grace," I said, hugging her.

"You're welcome," she said shyly.

Robert handed me his parcel next. "Here," he said. "Happy birthday, Vi!"

In his package was a copy of *Anne of Green Gables*, by L.M. Montgomery. My fingers tingled in excitement as I opened the book and took a peak at the first few pages. I had wanted to read this book for some time ever since I had seen it in the bookstore window.

"Thank you so much, Robby!" I said to him, smiling. "I can't wait to read it!" He grinned back at me.

"We're next," Helen said, coming forward with Anna. She handed me the large box and waited for me to open it, eyes shining with anticipation.

"Oh..." I said, upon opening the package. In the folds of brown paper lay a large journal, its cover decorated with dried, pressed flowers. Opening the journal, I found numerous pages of coarse paper on the inside—plenty of space to write. I stroked one of the petals with my fingertip, and smelled the paper—it smelled of roses. This would be the perfect place in which I could write all my thoughts.

"Thank you, Helen and Anna!" I said, hugging both of my sisters in turn.

"I believe there's one more," Mum said. She placed a small package in my hand.

"It's from both of us really, but your mother picked it out," Father added.

Pulling away the brown paper, I found a lovely pair of dark-red hair ribbons, shiny-new. Tears came to my eyes—Mum knew how much I loved the color red.

"Thank you, Mum and Father," I said. "I love them—I can't wait to wear them!"

"I'm glad you're pleased with them, dear," Mum said, smiling. She kissed my forehead softly.

After wishing me a happy birthday once more, Father gave Mum a quick goodbye kiss on the cheek, then left the apartment. He had a carpentry job that would take him all day.

"Well girls, we have chores to complete," Mum said briskly, standing up and brushing her skirt off. She collected all the sticky plates. "We'll leave you to get dressed, Vi," she added, leaving the room.

Once alone, I made my bed and got dressed. I took extra care with my curls this morning, twisting them up into a bun, and securing the bun with one of my new ribbons. The ribbons would always be a reminder of my generous family from that day forth—a family who was willing to spend all of their extra money and use all of their extra time to make my birthday special.

CHAPTER 22

Now that spring was really and truly here, I loved waking in the mornings to the warm sunlight streaming through my window. In the winter it was cold and dark, which always made me reluctant to rise in the morning. The warm spring sunshine almost seemed to say, "Come, get up! The day has begun!" And I would welcome the rays with open arms.

"Violet, please take the children out to run around a bit," Mum said a few days after my birthday. "Take care not to lose anyone." She smiled at me.

"I won't, Mum," I said assuredly.

"Good."

"Henry, Grace, I'm going to take you outside. We can go to the park," I said to them.

"Ooh, the park!" Grace squealed.

"Get your shoes and jackets on," Mum said firmly. "There is still a bit of a chill in the air; it's not yet summer, you know."

"Yes, Mum," Henry replied quickly. "Come Grace," he said, taking her arm and leading her to the bedroom.

I smiled after them, then turned and sat down at the table. "Oh Mum, I can hardly wait! Lilli is coming in less than a month. She will be here—we will be *neighbors*. It's more wonderful than anything of which I've ever dreamed."

"It seems you've had quite some time to think it over, though," Mum said. "Did it just now come to you now that Lillian will be here with us soon?"

"I'm not sure," I said thoughtfully. "I thought I was excited before, but now I'm even more excited. It's like my heart was filled with all the joy it could hold, and then it expanded to hold even more joy. I feel light as a bubble; I feel *free*."

"You haven't felt like that for a long time, have you, Vi?" Mum's eyes looked deep into mine, as though she could see my heart.

"No," I whispered.

"We've had a lot of trouble and hardship in this new home," Mum mused. "I haven't seen you this excited in quite a while." She kissed my forehead. "I'm glad you can experience joy once more."

Just then Henry entered the room. "Mum," he said. "Gracie can't find her other shoe."

"Oh dear," Mum said, wiping her hands on her worn apron. "Come, I'll help you find them." She took his hands and led him down the hall.

I fingered the apron that Mum had taken off. The holes were patched and thin; it was almost worn through.

Suddenly, I was reminded of a time when my sisters and I all wished to buy her a new apron together. But what with the factory, and then Mum's sickness, and all the business afterward with the ham and the holidays... well, I had forgotten.

"Mum needs a new apron," I said to myself. "And I'm going to get her one."

"Oh you are, are you?" Emma asked, smiling at me. I had forgotten that she was in the room, bent over her sewing in the corner.

270

"Indeed," I said solemnly. "Or at least I mean to try."

"I'll help you," Emma said, coming over from her chair. She laid a hand on my shoulder. "That way it will be easier for us to save up enough for the fabric. I think we should have enough, if we put our money together. Fabric isn't very expensive. We can purchase it sometime later this week," she added. "Oh, or better yet, you could get Ethan to buy it for us."

"How does that change things?"

"If we both go out, Mum will know something's up," she said. "If Ethan brings a package—maybe if he puts it on the doorstep when Mum's in the bedroom—then Mum will never know."

"Good idea," I mused. "Then in that case, I think we should tell Helen about our plan."

"Why?"

"First, she may be able to add some money to our fund," I said, counting off each reason on my hand. "Second, Helen has good ideas. She may suggest something of which we never thought. And third, Helen is extremely intelligent and will grow very suspicious,

271

even if Mum doesn't. She might tell Mum, and that would be bad. If she's in on the secret, she wouldn't tell Mum, because she'd know the plan."

"That's a good point," Emma said. "But I think we should naturally assume that if we tell Helen, Anna's in on the secret, too. You know that Helen tells everything to her twin."

Just then Mum entered the room, Henry and Grace with her.

"We found the shoe," she said.

"Good," I replied quickly, trying to act as though Emma and I had been speaking of something of little matter, such as the weather.

As though she could read my thoughts, Emma promptly spoke up.

"We were just discussing how lovely this spring weather has been as of late," she said lightly.

"Oh yes, it has been very nice, hasn't it?" Mum replied. She didn't seem to suspect anything amiss. I breathed out slowly through my mouth.

"Well, I'd best go take the children out," I said quickly. "Come Grace." I took her hand, and nodded for Henry to follow me.

"Watch out for automobiles as you cross the street!" Mum said.

"We will," I promised.

The street was crowded with the noisy automobiles, and it was quite dangerous, for they could easily run over a young child. Henry was fascinated with them, thinking it a wonder that people could travel from place to place without a horse and buggy, but I thought the whole business of them was silly. I much preferred riding a horse. Automobiles were one of the few things that always would bother me about the city; among others being the noise and the smells and the crowds.

"Watch out!" I cried, yanking Henry back by the collar of his shirt, to keep him from being hit by an automobile. The angry driver honked his horn at us as he screeched past us and on down the street.

"Take better care, Henry," I scolded him, when we were safely on the sidewalk once more.

"I wanted to see it..." he whined. "You never let me see automobiles up close."

"That's because they're dangerous!" I snapped back. "Mum instructed me to take care of you, and I have no wish to repeat the incident that occurred with Helen and the harbor."

"Do you have to bring *that* up again?" Henry asked, rolling his eyes. "It's getting a little old. Helen fell into the harbor almost three months ago."

"I don't care—that doesn't mean I'm going to be careless again!" I turned around and started walking backwards, facing Henry so that I could see his face.

"Violet..." Henry started to say.

"Listen to me," I said. "You need to learn that it's not good to run into—"

"People?"

I turned around instantly, realizing that I had just run into Ethan.

"Oh, I'm so sorry, Ethan," I stuttered, blushing. "I was just talking to Henry here about the seriousness of running into the street."

"Ah," Ethan said, leaning back on his heels with his hands in his pockets. "But it seems that, while you are giving excellent instruction to your brother about why you shouldn't run into the street, you saw no harm in running into *me*."

"It was an accident," I protested quickly. "And I feel very remorseful of it."

"I know, Violet—I really am not that bothered." He grinned. "Though... it was quite funny."

I rolled my eyes. "For you, perhaps!" I retorted.

"Fair enough," he said quickly. "Now, where were you going?"

"I was just taking Grace and Henry to the park," I explained. "Mum thought they needed to get their energy out."

"I see," he said, glancing at Grace, who was tugging on my hand. "Well then, I won't hold you up. Good day, Miss Bradshaw." And then he walked away, taking long strides.

"Can we go now, Violet?" Grace asked me, her little face full of pleading.

"Yes, of course," I answered.

Violets Are Blue

"Is there a letter for me?" I asked Emma, entering the apartment and removing my bonnet.

"Yes, there is," Emma replied. She handed me the envelope.

Dear Violet,

This shall be the last letter I write you for at least two weeks. Dearest, you shall have to bear it for I will be most busy and will simply not have the time to pen a note, much as I should wish. I shall be helping Mum with the packing, and then we will be traveling to Southampton... oh, I shall be extremely occupied. And, even though I will be unable to write you, you will still be in my thoughts at all times.

Once I am on the Titanic, however, I will be able to write many, many letters. I will have plenty of time, and I shall devote an hour a

276

day to writing you. How else am I to make up for the time that I couldn't write you? I think, though, that there may be one or two days that I do not write... but I can't help it! The ship sounds so beautiful, just from the descriptions in our newspaper. I can't even begin to think of the luxury... There will be so much for me to do. There is even a swimming pool and a gymnasium, some say. I am not sure if I would care to swim, but the gymnasium sounds fascinating. But perhaps those are only for first class... If that is the case, I will not be allowed in either. Oh, well. I did not wish to swim anyway. And this gives me more letter-writing time.

And when the ship docks... I shall see you! Oh Violet, it's been almost a year since you moved to America. I'm happy to say that I shall join you in just a few weeks. Ooh, I can't wait!

Love,

Lilli

"Violet?" Emma's voice interrupted my reading. "Violet!" she hissed.

"What?" I asked in alarm, looking about the kitchen. Everyone appeared to be elsewhere—the kitchen was empty.

"I have come up with a plan," she whispered.

"About what?" I asked curiously.

"About making an apron for Mum, you silly!" she said impatiently. "I have asked Ethan, and he said that it was perfectly all right with him. He's to purchase the fabric—with our money, of course—and give it to you when you're next at the butcher's."

"And then?"

"Well, perhaps we'll let Father in on our plan and he can arrange for Mum to be out of the apartment at that time... maybe at the park with the little ones."

"I just took them to the park today," I said to Emma. "How many times do they need to go?"

"Little children have a lot of energy," Emma replied smoothly. "Anyway, that part doesn't matter. Mum just has to be out of the apartment."

"And I will sneak the fabric inside?"

278

"Yes. You will take the package inside and hide it under our bed, perhaps... would that be a good hiding spot?"

"Yes, that works well enough," I said. "But how do we make the apron?"

"Oh, that part's easy," Emma said quickly. "We can take turns sewing in here, when Mum's in the kitchen. She often sends one of the children to call everyone to dinner anyway—it's not as if she were likely to enter our bedroom."

"Well, it sounds very good," I said slowly. "You've thought this out very well, Emma."

She beamed. "I just think it's a good surprise."

"And it will be," I said with certainty.

CHAPTER 23

"Only a week," I said one morning in early April.

"Only a week until what?" Anna asked me.

"Until Lilli's ship leaves port in Southampton," I explained. "We will see each other but five days after that. Only twelve more days."

"You'd best stop daydreaming and get back to work," Anna complained. "How am I to get this floor clean without your help? Mum said you were supposed to help me."

"I know, I know, I'm coming," I said slowly, getting up from my seat beside the window.

I dipped my rag into the bucket of soapy water and began to scrub the floor. Emma was in the other room—knitting—and Mum was taking a loaf of bread to a neighbor. The children were with Emma, playing with Henry's set of wooden blocks, and Milky was in his usual spot by the stove.

I sat back on my ankles after only five minutes of scrubbing. "You don't suppose there will be any... delays, do you?"

Anna sighed. "Vi..."

"Well, I was just wondering... Do you think the *Titanic* will arrive on schedule? Or will it be a bit detained?"

"How should I know?"

"You're right." I sighed. I felt as though I had many questions, and yet no one knew the answers.

"Vi, could you come here for a minute?" Emma requested from the bedroom.

I jumped up quickly, knocking the bucket of soapy water over in my haste. Anna groaned loudly.

"No need to help me—I can clean it up," she said sarcastically.

"Thanks, Anna," I said quickly, then walked to the bedroom door.

"What is it, Emma?"

"Vi, Mum's out—visiting a neighbor. Wouldn't this be the perfect time—"

"To get the fabric?" I asked, finishing her sentence. "I don't know... did Mum say we were allowed to go out of the apartment?"

"Well... if I were to stay with the children, I'm sure it would be fine," Emma said. "You can go fetch it from Mr. Hartley."

"I'll go now," I said, already halfway out the door.

"Go quickly," Emma said, handing me a covered basket.

"What's this?" I asked.

"Something in which you can carry the fabric. We don't want Mum to see it, no matter what."

"Perfect," I said. Emma was always so well prepared.

"Where is Vi going?" Grace asked suddenly.

"She's just going to... do a bit of shopping," Emma explained, lifting Grace onto her hip.

"Shopping?" Robert asked in surprise. "Do we need anything?"

"Yes, we do, and if I don't go to purchase it, we shall be at a loss for... it," I said vaguely.

282

Waving goodbye to the rest of the children—who still didn't know why I was leaving—I quickly departed.

Once outside, I took a deep breath. Despite the smells and sounds, I was glad to breathe fresh air. I breathed out slowly, then directed my steps toward the butcher shop.

"Good day, Miss Bradshaw," Ethan said, unusually formal. He glanced around to make sure his uncle was out of earshot, and then said, "I believe you are looking for this?" He held up a large package wrapped in brown paper and tied with string.

"Yes, thank you," I said my tone as formal as his. "It was so kind of you to pry yourself away from the shop long enough to do this for me, Mr. Hartley."

"It was no trouble," Ethan said. "Besides, I was glad to get away. The butcher shop isn't for me."

"Really?" I asked curiously. This was something I'd never expected him to say.

"Yes, well, I'm apprenticed to my uncle for about two more years. When my apprenticeship is over, I hope to move to New Hampshire, or Maine perhaps."

"What does your uncle think of this plan?"

"He doesn't know of it yet. All I know is that he is hopeful that I will continue to run the butcher shop after he dies, until *I* die, maybe." He shook his head. "The butchering business isn't for me." Then he leaned closer and whispered, "To tell you the truth, I'm not that fond of the city at all. What I love are the rushing waves coming onto the beach; the smell of the salt air..."

"All things that you have right here," I reminded him.

"Yes, but that's not what I mean," Ethan said. "I'm talking about living right by the waves, where it's not quite so crowded."

"Yes," I said, taking the package. "Good day, Ethan." I curtsied quickly, then went out the door.

"I got the—" I started to say, entering the apartment with my covered basket.

"You got what, Vi?" Mum asked. She was standing by the table, laying the top crust on an apple pie.

"Oh..." I said nervously. "I was just saying that I... got... plenty of fresh air while I was outside... uh, taking a walk."

"I see," Mum said. Her eyes seemed to see right into me.

"I'm going to go find Emma," I said quickly, then dashed away.

"Vi, what's in the basket?" Mum called after me, but I was already gone.

"Emma, I got it!" I gasped, entering the bedroom.

She glanced furtively around, then closed the door. "Did you say you got the fabric, Vi?" she asked, when we were alone.

"Yes," I said, removing the cloth from the basket. "Did you tell Ethan what we wanted?"

"I didn't know what to ask for," Emma said. "I just asked him to get something suitable for a woman's apron."

"Well, I hope it will work..." I said slowly, pulling back the brown paper from the package.

"Oh..." Emma said softly, staring at the fabric from over my shoulder.

The fabric was off-white—the color of fresh buttermilk. It was sprinkled with printed sprigs of wildflowers. The fabric was soft cotton—it felt lovely in my hands. It was perfect; I couldn't have selected it better myself.

"How did Ethan know..." I trailed off in amazement.

"This will work splendidly," Emma said, a smile on her pretty face.

"When shall we begin the sewing of it?"

"I think I will begin tomorrow morning. I shall rise early, before Mum is awake. I can cut out the pieces, at least, and then we can take turns sewing each morning."

"Yes, that's a good plan. We have to do it when Mum's not awake, for she's already suspicious of us..."

"She is?" Emma asked, looking alarmed. "Well, then we'd better put the fabric away for now."

She folded up the cloth and placed it back in my basket. I slid the basket under my bed, as we'd planned.
286

We both grinned as we entered the kitchen, for we loved planning surprises.

"What were you doing in the bedroom?" Henry asked curiously as we entered the kitchen.

"Emma was just showing me the... bed she made." I fumbled through the words, unable to think of an excuse on the spot.

"There was a hole in the quilt, and I was teaching her how to mend it without the seam showing," Emma added smoothly, winking at me.

"Oh yes, that's right," I said quickly.

"How did you manage to forget what you were doing just five minutes ago?" Helen asked skeptically.

"It was a very trying task," Emma whispered loudly to Helen, as though revealing a big secret. "Vi got distracted a lot—it's a wonder she didn't sew the sheet to the quilt!"

Anna grinned, but Helen still looked suspicious.

"Shall we eat?" Mum asked.

"Yes," Father said quickly. "Let us pray, children."

We all bowed our heads as Father prayed.

"Dear Lord, thank You for all the bounty You have lavished upon us. We are forever grateful for Your love and protection of our family. I ask that You grant the Prescotts a save voyage across the Atlantic, and I pray that we will be able to see all of their faces soon. Please bless this food to our bodies, and let it nourish us and give us strength. Amen."

"Amen," I said softly.

After supper was over, I saw Emma take Helen and Anna aside.

"I have something to tell you, girls," she whispered.

CHAPTER 24

Lilli's arrival was to be any day now. I couldn't stand the waiting, for I had never been one for patience. The very thought of seeing my best friend again in person after nearly a year away from her sent chills of delight down my spine. I couldn't sit still; I always had to be doing something, or otherwise the waiting would drive me mad.

"Mum, may I go down to the harbor?" I requested one evening after dinner. I reflected later that I sounded exactly like Robert, always begging to see the ships.

"Not tonight—it's far too late," Mum said. "If the *Titanic* had arrived, we would have heard about it. You must bide your time."

"But Mum..." I pleaded.

"No 'buts', Violet Elisabeth Bradshaw. I won't have you trying to wheedle me into allowing you, when I strictly told you 'no.'"

"Yes, ma'am." I sighed. I trudged down the hall to the bedroom, where Emma was sewing Mum's apron.

"Help me please, Violet," she requested. "I need you to pin this pocket here."

I helped her pin the fabric, all the while pouring out my frustration.

"She knows how excited I am to see Lilli just as soon as I possibly can, and yet she holds me back here. It's awful."

"Violet, if the *Titanic* had arrived, we would have heard about it," Emma answered patiently, echoing my mother's words. "As Mum said, you must exercise patience. Lilli and her family will arrive on time, and we will all go to greet them... *when the ship arrives.* Now, hand me that spool of thread, please."

I handed the thread to her, my jaw set in a frown. I couldn't stand anymore of this waiting, no matter how much Mum and Emma thought I needed to be patient.

"I think I'll read," I said to Emma, taking *Anne of Green Gables* from the table beside my bed.

"Very well," Emma consented.

I had been reading but ten minutes when I heard footsteps coming from the kitchen, and then Robert's voice.

"Mum!" he gasped. "There's a big commotion down at the harbor! Something about the *Titanic!*"

My heart beat rapidly.

"Really?" Mum asked quizzically. "That's strange. Now Vi, wait one minute—"

But she was too late. I had already flown from the bedroom, through the kitchen, and out of the apartment door. My feet pounded down the stairs, my sides heaving. All I could think of was seeing Lilli.

The harbor had never seemed farther; my feet had never moved so slowly. The wind beat against me, holding me back. Despite the fact that it was April, the evening air was cool, but I paid no attention to the chilly breeze. I ran with lightning in my steps. People stared at me as I ran, but I moved right past them.

Violets Are Blue

Why were the roads so long tonight? Why couldn't my feet move more rapidly? I couldn't contain my excitement; this was the moment for which I had waited several months.

A large crowd had gathered around the harbor. I saw a ship docked, but it was somewhat smaller than the pictures of the *Titanic* Robert saved from the newspapers.

That's odd, I thought.

But I was given no more time to speculate it. As people poured forth from this ship, I finally saw the name painted on the side: R.M.S. *Carpathia*.

How could that be? Was another ship to arrive; a ship of which I was not aware? Fear started to seep through my bones. What had happened to the *Titanic*?

A young boy stood by the piers, waving a newspaper over his head. I caught a glimpse of the headline and froze. The sickening words were bolded and large:

THE TITANIC SINKS WITH ONLY 1,800 ON BOARD; ONLY 675, MOSTLY WOMEN AND CHILDREN, SAVED.

292

It was as though someone had shoved a stake into my heart.

My mind went blank. I couldn't breathe. My lips kept repeating the word "no," over and over and over again, but no sound came from my throat. My chest felt tight; my muscles incapable of moving. A horrible ache, far worse than any I'd ever felt before, gripped my heart.

It was impossible; unreal; too *cruel* to be true. All my waiting, all my hoping, for nothing? Only to find out that she was dead. My best friend was dead. And I didn't even get to say goodbye.

I never should have left Eastbourne. It was all my fault that Lilli was dead, her lifeless body at the bottom of the freezing ocean. If I had stayed, she never would have had reason to come to America in the first place. I was the cause for my friend's death.

I remained by Pier 54 for hours. The rain poured down on me, soaking my clothes and my hair. I barely felt the drops. The sky grew dark. I didn't even notice people leaving, until I was the only one by the pier.

Violets Are Blue

I sat huddled on the damp ground, my arms wrapped around my knees. It was too dark; I couldn't see very well. Not that I cared. I would stay here, out in the rain, until I was sick. I didn't care if I died. Lillian was dead, after all—why shouldn't I be as well?

"Violet!"

Someone had called my name. I heard footsteps over the constant downpour of the rain.

It was Ethan.

"Violet, what are you doing here?" he asked, staring at my soaked clothing. "Your whole family is worried sick; we didn't know where you were."

"Did you hear about the *Titanic*, Ethan?" I asked him, my voice dull and flat.

"Oh no," he said, suddenly realizing. "Lilli. Uncle Wallace. I had forgotten."

"It sank, Ethan," I said bitterly. "Less than half of the passengers survived."

"I heard," he answered in a low voice. "It's a terrible tragedy. People were at the butcher shop talking about it this evening."

"And what did they say?" I demanded.

294

"They all said that it was a horrible tragedy, and that it seemed so unlikely. The newspapers advertised the ship as unsinkable, and everyone believed them."

"Unsinkable!" I scoffed bitterly. "Unsinkable! How foolish I was to believe that! And now my best friend's gone."

"You don't know that, Violet," Ethan said softly. "Perhaps she's gone to stay in a boarding house with her family, and she'll come to your apartment tomorrow..."

"You don't understand, Ethan! She's *gone*," I said through clenched teeth. "And it's all my fault. I'll never see her again."

"But Violet..."

"I'm not in the mood to be comforted, Ethan. Leave me alone!" I turned my back.

"I can't, Violet. Your mother sent me to find you. I guess she thought you'd listen to me better than anyone else."

"Well, she was wrong," I said stubbornly.

"Then there's clearly only one thing to do," Ethan replied calmly. "If you won't listen to reason, I will have to resort to force." He started to take my arm.

"Let go of me!" I screamed. My haunting shriek echoed back in the dark night, full of heartbreaking despair.

"Violet, you can't stay out here all night alone."

"I can if I want to," I replied curtly. I knew how ridiculous I sounded, but I did not feel like listening to reason at the moment.

"Fine," Ethan replied, just as curtly. "As you wish." He started to walk away.

"Oh, all right!" I replied quickly, before I lost sight of his retreating figure. No matter how stubborn I was, I didn't care to sleep out of doors on tonight of all nights.

"Good, you're being reasonable," Ethan said, as I fell into step beside him.

"I'm only coming with you because it's far too damp a night for anyone to be outside, and because I don't wish to cause my family worry. If it weren't for those things, I would absolutely refuse to come."

"I am aware of that," Ethan answered. "I'm just glad that you're safe."

We walked in silence for a while, until we reached the apartment building.

"Well, here we are," Ethan said. "Do you want me to escort you in?"

"I know how to get into my own family's apartment, Ethan Hartley," I snapped.

"Very well then," he consented. Nodding to me, he added, "Goodnight, Violet."

I trudged up the stairs to my apartment, my shoulders shaking from cold. I had just raised my hand to knock on the door when Emma opened it.

"Oh Violet," she said, taking in my dripping clothes and hair. "Come inside, dear." She called out, "Mum, Violet's home!"

"Oh Violet, you frightened us so," Mum said, coming into the kitchen. "I just prayed that Ethan would find you."

"I don't see how it was any big secret where I was," I said sullenly. I didn't feel like being pleasant.

"We heard about the *Titanic*, Vi," Emma said, tears coming to her eyes. "Do you think the Prescotts are really gone for good, Mum? Do you think we can have any hope that they survived?"

"We can most certainly hope," Mum said. "We must have faith that God is watching over them, whether they be alive or..."

"Dead," I finished flatly.

"Yes, well, we were all very worried about you," Mum said quickly. "Come, get a hot bath, dear—we don't want you catching cold."

I followed her to the table, where I sat down, my clothes dripping on the floor and forming a puddle.

"I was already heating water," Mum said softly. "I knew you'd be wet, what with this rain we had. Here," she poured it into a large tub, "let's get you warmed up."

After my bath, I crawled into bed, dressed warmly in a long nightgown and stockings. Mum kissed me goodnight softly, then left the room. I was left in the dark, alone with my thoughts. And it was then that I began to truly weep.

My tears came in torrents; for a while, I was almost scared that I'd never be able to stop them. I wept uncontrollably; I was beyond all comfort. My shoulders

298

shook bitterly, and still I wept on, my pillow growing soaked from my tears.

Gasping, my tears finally ran out. And it was then that the ache reasserted itself, claiming space in my heart once more. I wanted to shove it out, but it was something that, somehow, could not be defeated. A huge lump was in my throat, and I couldn't swallow it, no matter how hard I tried.

I had never felt pain like this; this hurt, this loneliness, this emptiness. I had thought my heart was broken before, but I realized now that I had been mistaken. *This* was a broken heart. In fact, my heart was more than broken; it was *gone*. All that was left was emptiness where my heart had once been.

A part of me seemed to die when the *Titanic* went down to her watery grave.

CHAPTER 25

I awoke in the morning with a bad headache, but I pushed myself to get out of bed. All eyes — Emma's, Mum's, Helen's, Anna's, and even Grace's — seemed to be on me. They were all waiting for some sign of great sadness. I didn't intend to show any.

I had learned through experience that, in times of great trial, if one is to show one's emotions she will receive pity. I did not want pity. And so, I hid all of my emotions behind a wall of ice, blocking out all feelings. I was careful not to let that wall melt, building it up once more if needed. It helped some, but the downside was that it took away any little bit of happiness I had left.

I pushed myself to appear normal; to do what was expected of me. I even sewed for an hour one day, without a word of complaint. I didn't dare show any sign of my bruised and broken heart. It stayed hidden behind my self-imposed wall, impossible to reach.

Mum and Emma were worried, I could tell. I was always obedient, always helpful; in fact, I was more obedient and helpful than I had been before. But I could sense that was not what concerned them.

They were worried about my heart. They were worried that I would grow bitter and resentful for the rest of my life. They wanted me to open up about my pain and sorrow; they wanted to comfort me. The whole family felt sadness over the loss of the Prescotts, but they sought comfort in each other. I had no one to whom I could tell my fears.

I wept in silence each night, after the family was asleep. This went on for about a week, until I found I could cry no longer. My eyes were dry, and all that remained was a deep, painful ache where my heart had once been. I longed to wash it away with tears and comfort, but it was too late. I wouldn't let my ice wall down for a moment; I didn't even know if I *could* let it down now, even if I had wanted, for it was so tall and so thick. I had wanted my wall to grow, and grow it did. I couldn't go back; I couldn't change it now. I was simply left with the consequences.

Mum made oatmeal for breakfast that first morning. I ate mine slowly, wishing I could swallow the lump in my throat as easily as I swallowed the oatmeal. I didn't know how to get rid of it. It certainly wasn't something for which you could go to the doctor's. He would think I had gone crazy.

"Violet..." Emma asked me, her wary voice breaking into my thoughts.

I jumped, realizing that I had been sitting, staring into the distance, my spoon froze in midair.

"What's wrong with Vi?" Henry asked innocently.

"Nothing," Mum and Emma said quickly, in perfect unison.

"Eat your oatmeal, Henry," Father instructed, "before it gets cold."

"But—" he started to protest.

"Eat." Father's voice was stern, and Henry finally obeyed.

"You don't look well, Vi," Helen observed, looking at me with concern. Grace and Anna were both staring at me as well, their eyes worried. Robert was the

302

only one who seemed unconcerned as he diligently ate his oatmeal.

"I'm—I'm fine," I said shakily, despite the fact that I didn't *feel* fine. My headache was worse, and I felt a sick feeling in the pit of my stomach.

"Violet, go lie down," Mum instructed firmly.

"That's not fair! Why does she get out of cleaning the kitchen?" Helen whined.

"Helen," Father said. His tone was no-nonsense.

"Mum, I'm fine—" I tried to protest, but she shook her head firmly.

"You need to lie down. I'll help the girls clean up the kitchen."

I didn't dare protest any further, so I left the table and went to my bedroom. Lying down on my bed, I tried to keep the room from spinning around me. I didn't succeed.

Mum came in about ten minutes later to check on me and I was faced with the grim fact: I was sick.

I was in bed for nearly three days with a fever. For once, I didn't want to get up—I was happy to rest. Every time I tried to sit up, I'd get so dizzy that I'd have to lie back down again. The hours passed without my knowing, and it was hard to keep track of the days. I drifted in and out of consciousness. Helen grudgingly brought me my meals each day, complaining that she wasn't my maid, but she never failed to complete her task on schedule.

During my illness I had a lot of time to think. And all that free time scared me. Alone with my thoughts, with no other responsibilities at hand, I began to think more and more about Lilli. The pain overwhelmed me; it was as if I was in the middle of the ocean, with a weight tied around my feet. I pulled and struggled, gasping for air, but the weight just kept pulling me down, further and further and further. I knew I would eventually hit the bottom.

"No!" I screamed, sitting up straight in bed.

Looking around, I realized that it was the middle of the night. Mum had blown out all the candles long ago. The room was silent, as was the one next door. Did I awake anyone with my scream?

No, everyone was still sleeping soundly. I lay back down and tried to fall asleep again, but somehow I

304

couldn't. I was lonely; a little girl with a broken heart. I wanted Mum to kiss my forehead and tell me things were going to be fine.

But I couldn't. I couldn't tell her what was going on, especially after I'd refused any comfort or help for so long. Besides, things *weren't* going to be fine. Mum might be good at soothing me, but she certainly couldn't bring people back to life.

I slept restlessly that night, tossing and turning. I was exhausted when morning finally showed her face between the grey clouds.

Slowly, wearily, I got better. I regained my strength, and often sat in the rocking chair in the kitchen while the others worked, busy as bees. I tried to knit, but found I had no desire any more. Life seemed to have lost its color.

I was glad when Mum finally pronounced me well enough to go outside. I had gone so long without seeing the sun... it seemed almost like a distant memory. I put my bonnet on and tied the ribbons quickly. My cheeks were still a bit pale, but other than that, I felt fine.

Joy, of course, was unlikely, but it would be nice to get some fresh air.

I strolled down the street at a leisurely pace, not really going anywhere in particular. I spotted Mary outside her father's forge, and she waved to me. I waved halfheartedly back.

"Hello, Vi!" she said to me cheerfully. "I see you're well once more."

"Yes, Mum declared me fit, so I decided to take a bit of a walk," I said.

"Well, that's good."

We stood in silence for a moment, not knowing what to say.

"I'm... sorry about your friend," she said suddenly, her tone soft.

"I don't know what you're talking about."

"Lillian, your friend who was coming to America on the *Titanic*."

"Why should you be sorry about her?" I asked coldly.

"Didn't she... die?" Mary asked. She seemed reluctant to say the words.

306

Elizabeth Rose

"Yes, yes, of course she did. What, did you think she would *survive?*" My tone was bitter.

"Well, like I said, I'm awfully sorry." She seemed uncertain what else to say, so strange and different was my tone of voice.

"I'd best be going," I said stiffly. "Good day, Mary."

I walked further down the street, past the shops and towards the harbor. I didn't want to run into anyone else I might know; anyone who would try to comfort me. I certainly was not going to be comforted.

Finally, I reached the harbor. Standing on the edge of one of the piers, I started at the ocean. It seemed to stretch on and on, without any ending. It looked so vast and deep and *lonely.* I couldn't bear it—seeing the waters stretching before me like this, without an end, broke my heart. Somewhere out there, in all that vastness, on the ocean floor, lay my best friend.

"LILLI!!!!!!" I screamed. No response. Only the echo of my voice, bouncing back over the endless waves, empty and lonely.

I couldn't stay for long, otherwise I would break down in tears. So I turned, slowly, woodenly, and made my way back to the apartment building where my family was waiting.

The days and then weeks wore by, slow and monotonous. It made me angry that they continued in this fashion; I almost felt as if the world should have ended after the *Titanic* sank. *That* would assure me that my sadness and anger was justified. But no, the world didn't end. It just kept going, on and on and on, an endless stream of dull days and terrible, sleepless nights. The clock's hands moved slowly, steadily.

I saw Lilli in my dreams. She was always coming towards me, a smile on her face. And then... she'd fade away. And I'd wake up, only to find out that it all had been a dream. It was the worst feeling in the world. Each dream broke my heart more, making me sink deeper into depression. False hope was the predator and I the helpless prey.

Elizabeth Rose

It just didn't seem fair. Why did *she* die? What was wrong with *her*? What did she do to deserve this awful punishment?

I should have been punished. *I* should have been on that ship; *I* should have been the one who was killed. She didn't deserve to die... but I did.

The more I thought about it, the more it made sense. Lilli had been killed for no reason. I was the guilty one; I was the one to be blamed. And I was here, alive, while she was dead. It wasn't just, and if there was anything I hated, it was an injustice. God had killed her for no reason, at least no reason that I could understand. As far as I was concerned, He had made a mistake.

There was clearly only one thing to be done. *I* had to die. Maybe if I was dead, God would accept me as compensation for all that I had done wrong.

All I had to do was die.

As soon as I had made up my mind, other matters were fairly simple. The harbor was deep—I could just throw myself in. I wondered how long it would take for me to drown. I'd have to ignore the natural instinct to swim back to the pier, and simply let myself go. But other than that, how hard could it be?

With my resolve firm in place, I walked briskly through the kitchen and outside. Mum was in her bedroom, changing the bed sheets, and Emma was in the kitchen with the children. They looked up as I went out, but didn't say anything, assuming, I guessed, that I was taking a walk.

Well, that's all I was doing—taking a walk. A walk that was leading me to my self-imposed death.

Mr. O' Neale was whistling in his forge, and other shopkeepers were cheerfully sweeping the sidewalk in front of their stores, or arranging goods in the shop windows. None of them paid any attention to me.

When I reached the harbor, I paused for a moment. The water looked so *deep*. I temporarily had forgotten my fear and dislike of deep water. It had seemed so *easy* back at home; where was that comfortable assurance now? I was having second thoughts.

I couldn't stay alive! It wasn't fair! I deserved to *die*.

310

And, with that thought in mind, I dove into the cold water.

I was all tense for the chilling rush I had anticipated upon hitting the surface of the water, when I realized something:

Someone was holding my arm, yanking me back.

What?! No! This was wrong! This wasn't my plan! Oh, *why* did everything always happen to me?

These thoughts flashed through my head as I turned slowly on my heels, expecting to see Father, or perhaps Ethan, behind me.

Instead, a tall lad whom I didn't recognize at first stood behind me on the pier, yanking me to safety.

His hair was dark. His eyes were grey and serious, and they looked at me with confusion and then surprise. He opened his mouth to speak.

"Violet, what on earth are you *doing?*"

It was Will Prescott.

Realization hit me suddenly. Will was here! He was alive! But how could that be?

I was whirled into a hurricane of sudden emotions. He was here—did that mean Lilli was here, too? Was she alive? Oh, *why* was I just standing here?

Will was still looking at me with an odd expression in his eyes. I remembered that I had failed to answer his question.

"Oh, I... um..." I didn't know what to say. *"I was trying to drown, Will,"* was certainly not the way to begin a conversation, especially with someone you haven't seen for almost a year.

"Why were you jumping into the harbor?" he asked me shrewdly.

I was tempted for a moment to tell him that harbor-swimming was a great sport here, but then realized the nonsense in such a statement. Besides, he would soon find out that I had not told him the truth, and then what would I say?

"I... fell," I said weakly. "Or at least I was falling. Until you came and rescued me."

"I'm glad to be of service," he said, removing his hat and bowing.

I curtsied in response, grinning.

312

"Will, where is the rest of your family?" I asked him quickly, looking about.

"Um... not right now, Miss Bradshaw," he said quickly. "There will be plenty time for explanations later. For now, I must see you safely to your home."

"This way," I said, pointing towards our street. "It's not very far."

As we walked, we talked little. I wondered why Will was so silent and solemn. He used to be so merry and jolly back when we all still lived in Eastbourne, always joking with Lilli and me. He seemed somewhat changed now.

"Will, what is it?" I asked finally, breaking a long silence.

"All in due time, Miss Bradshaw," was all he said.

I bit my tongue for the rest of the walk, convinced I wasn't going to be able to get anymore out of him.

Reaching the apartment, I turned to my companion. "Won't you come in? My parents would love to see you again after so long."

He smiled, but slowly shook his head. "I'm much obliged, Miss Bradshaw, but I can't right now. I have some business to which I must attend. Lucky I happened to be near the harbor when you most needed my assistance."

"And much obliged I am to you for saving me," I said politely. "It was such a blessing that you happened to be there at the right moment." I shuddered a little, thinking of what could have happened if he hadn't come so soon.

"But I'll be back," Will said cheerfully. "And then you will get your explanation."

CHAPTER 26

I dashed up the dirty stairs to our apartment, excited to share the good news with my family. I couldn't remember the last time I had felt this happy, but I didn't want it to go away. Weeping at night was certainly not a memory I wanted to think of, much less relive.

Emma was in the kitchen, drying wet dishes.

"Violet!" she gasped, taking in my windblown curls and eager eyes. "What's happened?"

"Emma... Emma..." I couldn't seem to spit out the words.

"Yes, what is it?" she asked impatiently.

"Emma, Will Prescott's alive!"

She stared at me, speechless. The joy in her eyes was mixed with complete shock. The dish she was drying slipped between her fingers and crashed to the floor, shattering in a hundred pieces.

"Violet," she said slowly, her voice sounding strained. "Are... are you *sure*?" Her eyes were incredulous.

"Of course I'm sure!" I exclaimed. "What? Are there other dark-haired English lads named Will Prescott walking around this city that I don't know of?"

"No, no," she said softly, sitting down in a chair. "I... I just couldn't believe it. You're sure it's him?"

"Yes!" I replied.

"And what about the rest of the family?" she demanded.

"He wouldn't say," I said slowly, somewhat confused.

"Oh," Emma said, her eyes downcast.

"What?" I asked, not understanding.

"Perhaps... perhaps he was the only one to survive."

"But that makes no sense!" I objected. "Women and children are always allowed in the lifeboats first. Will is a grown man—he's nineteen years old! His chances of survival are less than Lilli or Emily or Mrs. Prescott!"

316

"I can't explain it either," she said, her brow furled in puzzlement.

Henry bounced into the room at that moment, his eyes alight.

"Emma, Helen said—" His voice stopped abruptly, and he looked at me in confusion. "Violet, are you all right?" he asked me.

"Yes, I'm fine, Henry—why do you ask?"

"You just seem so... *happy.*" He looked perplexed at my joyful mood.

"Well, why wouldn't I be?" Was there some law of which I was not aware that banned all happiness?

"I don't know. You've been so sick... and sad."

I realized with a pang that my earlier depression had affected the rest of the family. While I wallowed in my own emotion, I had been immune to the fact that my family must have walked on eggshells around me, trying not to upset me further. How terribly I'd acted! Lillian's death was something that none of us could have changed, but my behavior in response to it was shameful.

"I'm sorry, Henry," I said, my tone apologetic. I approached him slowly, and leaned down until my face was level with his. "Will you forgive me?"

"For what?" he asked.

"For behaving in such a horrid manner. I'm sure I was awful."

"No, you weren't awful," he said, grinning. "Mum said that I would probably act the same way if my best friend died."

"Either way, it wasn't right of me to behave in such a manner. Will you forgive me?" I repeated.

"Of course," Henry replied eagerly. "I'm just glad you're happy again."

I hugged him fiercely, tears coming to my eyes.

"Vi, why didn't you ask Will to come inside?" Emma asked abruptly, as if the thought had just occurred to her.

"I asked, but he refused to come."

"Oh," she commented softly. Her voice sounded disappointed.

"I'm sure he'll come back," I added quickly. "Why wouldn't he? We're the closest thing to family he has here in America, after all."

"Yes, but perhaps he doesn't want to see us, no matter how close we were in Eastbourne." She looked at me, her eyes sad. "Things change. We haven't seen the Prescotts for so long. Perhaps..."

"Emma!" I exclaimed incredulously. "You can't possibly be suggesting that Will Prescott doesn't want to see us! Why, that's just ridiculous!"

"We have chores to do," she said suddenly, changing the subject. "Do you feel well enough to wield a broom?"

"Of course," I said quickly, getting up from my seat at the table. "And Emma?"

"Yes?"

"I still think Will wants to see you."

She blushed. "Don't suggest things, Vi. Your imagination easily gets out of hand sometimes." But she looked pleased, and her cheeks remained pink for a good while.

The day passed slowly, very slowly. I did my chores with half of my usual spirit, stopping every half hour to check the window. Will never came.

I had related to Mum all that had happened down by the harbor, leaving out my suicidal attempts. She seemed to believe me, but as the day progressed and Will still didn't come, she grew skeptical.

"Violet, are you sure he said he would come today?" she asked me at about five o' clock in the evening. "Perhaps you misunderstood his meaning."

"Well... he didn't exactly say he would come tonight... but he said he would *come*. I'm fairly certain he meant tonight."

She sighed, shook her head slowly, and turned back to her mending.

The hours ticked by. Suppertime came, and we ate by ourselves; we cleaned up together; Father read our evening devotions, and still no sign of Will.

Father was reading Proverbs chapter fourteen this evening, and he was just reading aloud the twenty-ninth verse when the clock chimed nine o' clock—bedtime.

"Come girls," Mum said, lifting a sleepy Grace into her arms. "Say goodnight to your father. It's time you get to bed. You too, boys." She nodded towards Henry and Robert, who quickly went to change into their nightclothes.

"Mum, can't I stay up and read just a bit longer?" I asked pleadingly.

"No, Vi," she said firmly. "You need your rest just as much as the other children."

Reluctantly, I stood and went to Father to say goodnight.

"Sleep well, Violet," he said, kissing my forehead.

"Goodnight, Father," I said in response. Then I went to change into my nightgown.

I had finished brushing my hair and was about to blow out the candle when I heard a knock at the door. I jumped in alarm, dropping my brush.

"Who could that be?" Mum asked softly, standing. She had just finished tucking Grace into bed.

Only one person could possibly come to visit at this hour.

Running through the kitchen in my bare feet, I threw open the door.

I was right.

"Will Prescott?" Mum asked, coming into the room.

"My children are going to sleep, lad. Why did you come so late?" Father asked sternly.

"I'm sorry," Will apologized, ducking his head. "I didn't mean to be a bother. I'll come back in the morning."

"No, no, come in, come in," Father insisted. "Sit down. Kathleen, could you get him a cup of tea?" he asked Mum, who went to boil the water.

Suddenly, the quiet kitchen was bustling with activity. I took down a china teacup and spooned honey into the bottom, while Mum poured the tea over the honey. Stirring it, she handed it to Will, who smiled gratefully and took a careful sip.

322

"Now," Father said, lighting his pipe. "I don't know where to begin. We haven't seen you in so long. How have you been?"

"Quite well, sir," Will replied. "That is, in health."

"Where is the rest of your family?" Father asked.

"That's what I came to speak about." His voice was sad. "They're dead, sir. I was the only one to survive the sinking."

"Oh Will, I'm so sorry," Mum said sympathetically.

"Thank you, Mrs. Bradshaw," he said.

I noticed that Emma had slowly crept out of the bedroom, a shawl wrapped around her arms. She squeezed my hand. I looked up into her eyes, and saw they were glowing with happiness. I almost wished I could feel as happy as she did... but I couldn't. Lilli wasn't here. She had died after all. I had gotten my hopes up for nothing. I prepared for the lump to reassert itself in my throat.

Will spoke again. "I think... I think perhaps I should tell you what happened... that night."

"Are you sure?" Mum asked him gently. "Don't try, if you're not ready."

"No, no," Will insisted. "I want you to know. I want Violet to know."

My eyes widened. What was he saying?

"It was the night of April fourteenth. It was almost midnight, and I was in my bed, asleep. Suddenly, I felt this large jolt and the ship seemed to scrape against something, something that I could not see. Lilli went to ask Mum and Father what had happened, but they thought it was a mere jolt and said that there was nothing to fear. Relieved, we both went back to our beds and swiftly fell asleep. Emily still slept soundly all the while— the jolt did not awaken her.

"Unfortunately, we were right to worry. Things were not right. About an hour later, I awoke to hear many voices out in the hallway.

" 'What in the world?' Father said, his voice groggy. He opened the door, nightclothes and all, and asked a passing steward, 'Is anything wrong?'

" 'Um... we seem to have had a bit of a scrape,' he said, reluctant to reveal the whole story.

324

" 'Tell them the truth!' a young mother said. She was carrying a baby and had two other children by her side. 'We've hit an iceberg, sir,' she said, talking to Father. 'The ship's a'sinkin'.'

"*Sinking?!* It couldn't be so. But it was the truth. Father urgently told us to grab one or two small necessities, and then to follow him.

" 'We must go to the deck and get into the lifeboats before they're all gone,' he insisted firmly. Suddenly I realized that this was a matter of life or death.

"We made our way to the deck as best we could, knee-deep in sea water. Men, women, and children swarmed around us, all speaking different tongues in anxious voices. I shoved my way past them, trying not to lose Father in the crowd. My body felt frozen and stiff, but we pushed through. Father carried Emily so that she wouldn't have to get as wet as the rest of us.

"Finally we reached the deck. By now, I could tell that the boat was sinking; the bow was sliding farther in the water, and the stern was rising up in the air. I saw passengers all slipping on the icy deck and sliding down the steep slope of the ship. Their screams were the most chilling of all sounds; I'll never forget the sound of their helpless, desperate voices, calling out in the dark night.

"There was one lifeboat left, a collapsible one. It was crowded with people. I ran towards it, nearly slipping on the icy deck, only to see the last lifeboat lowered into the water. We'd reached it too late.

" 'We'll have to jump,' Father said grimly.

" 'But Father!' Lilli started to protest.

" 'Lillian, there's no other option,' Father insisted firmly. 'We must jump now. If the stern gets too high in the air, our chances of survival will lessen. To jump from such a height would be... fatal.'

Here Will paused, and looked around the room. I could see the sadness in his eyes as he relived these horrible memories.

"You don't have to go on," Emma said softly, concerned for him.

"No, no, I'm fine," he insisted, forcing a smile onto his face. "Well, we jumped, and the impact when we hit the water was... terrible. We splashed about in the water for a while, each trying to grab onto something—a chair or a table, perhaps—anything to keep us as much

326

out of the water as was possible. It was the icy cold ocean that was the most fatal part.

"For hours, men, women, and children called out from the freezing water for help. Then slowly, everything began to grow silent. The passengers stopped screaming; the children stopped crying; for a while we all spoke not a word."

"Hours later, lights appeared in the distance, heralding the arrival of another ship and our rescuers. We were lifted over the side of the ship—she was called *Carpathia*—by hammocks and slings, and promptly given hot drinks and warm blankets. Many of the *Carpathia*'s passengers had given up their rooms so that we could have beds. They were extremely kind and generous.

"My family was tended to, but I knew they wouldn't live long. Emily was the first to pass away, followed by Mum, and then Father. Lilli was the last.

" 'Will, can you do me a favor?' she asked me one day, when I was sitting by her bed on the *Carpathia*.

" 'Anything,' I said quickly.

" 'Here, Will.' She pressed something into my hand.

" 'What is it?' I asked her.

" 'A letter,' she said softly. 'It's for Vi. Please give it to her if I don't... if I don't survive.'

" 'Lilli, I—'

" 'Do you promise, Will? Promise me you'll give it to her.'

" 'I promise,' I said.

" 'Give it to Vi,' she repeated. 'Give it to her.'

" 'Why can't you give it to her yourself?' I asked. 'You'll be well enough.'

" 'No,' she said quietly. 'No, I won't.' She turned to look me in the eye. 'I'm dying, Will.'

" 'You're going to get better, Lilli,' I said firmly.

" 'Will,' she said softly. 'I know I'm dying. I want you to give that letter to Violet. It explains everything. I want her to know I'm not sad. I don't want her to blame herself for my death in any way. I want her to know I'm going to see Jesus.'

"All I could do was nod. How could I refuse my sister anything at this moment?

"She passed away in her sleep that night."

Will sat quietly for a while, looking down into the palms of his hands, as if embarrassed to be the bearer of bad news. None of us spoke for a moment, taking everything in that he had said. It was just so much tragedy in one night—my brain could hardly wrap around it all. But the ship *had* sunk, and Lilli *had* died. I never would have heard the story behind it if it weren't for Will. He had lived, while the rest of his family died. Did God have Will survive for a reason we had yet to discover?

Suddenly, the silence was interrupted by Will. Pulling a battered envelope from his pocket, he handed it to me.

"Here, Violet," he said. It was Lilli's last letter.

I grasped the envelope. My fingers were trembling. Picking at it nervously so as not to rip it, I slowly unfolded the letter and drank in every word.

When finished, I carefully closed the letter and placed it gently back in the envelope. Looking up, I realized that my whole family was staring at me intently. Perhaps they thought I would start weeping uncontrollably or retreat once more into that horrid stony silence.

I delicately placed the letter into the pocket of my nightgown.

Helen broke the silence abruptly.

"What did the letter say, Vi?"

I hesitated. Then, turning to Helen, my heart began to beat.

"I'll tell you someday."

And slipping my hand into my pocket, I gently squeezed the folded pages.

Made in United States
North Haven, CT
10 March 2024

49656890R00211